To Be Saved

The second book in the To Be Loved series

To Be Saved Miranda Kruse © **2015**
All rights reserved.

I want to dedicate this book and thank all the brave men and women in the armed forces around the world who fight for the rights and freedom of others. To those who believe in being more than just heroes and who give their lives freely for the cause of keeping us all safe: Thank You!

I would also like to thank my personal heroes who made this book what it is today. Luke Deal and Caitlynn Fichtner. Without both of you I would still be lost.

Prologue:

When someone loses the most important person in the world to them, the grieving processes never ends. The presence of that one special person's existence, so dominate in their lives, ceases to exist. The trauma that causes to a person's daily life, effects the way they think, the way they move, the way they exist.

Every single day that person wishes, day dreams, and longs with a lonely, heart-broken spirit, that they could have just one more moment, one more hug, one more kiss from the person that meant the world to them.

To a soldier: one who is bound by honor and duty to protect the lives and freedom of his country and his home. The loss of a love so true and deep can be devastating to his ability to serve in what he believes is his path in life.

Chapter One: Going Back

June 2015
Luna Pier, Michigan
Merk Funeral Home

Darryl Krause walked into the funeral home where his entire family was gathered for the funeral of his uncle, full of anxiety and not ready to be here at all. His towering six foot three height and military build gave him a sense of unease over the crowd he was looking over and made it hard for him to stand in the entrance of the parlor without being noticed by everyone in the room.

Not that anyone was looking at him currently, he thought off handedly. Everyone in the room was gathered together in the front of the room near his uncle's casket.

Darryl's crisp clean, Army-green dress uniform adorned with medals of Honor and rank, all the way down to his dress boots made him feel more uncomfortable than he had ever felt around anyone in the presence of what should feel familiar to him.

He thought that nothing about being here felt familiar to him anymore. He had been gone from this place too long for that. Now, he's returned to his family a changed man, and this place had changed more since the last time he was here.

He had to admit though, it wasn't so much his military persona, or his height, he thought trying to convince himself otherwise, which always did make him feel uncomfortable around normal people, as much as it was his own stress disorder. He was fine in the Army, he was fine in war, and he was fine abroad, where he had been for twelve years. He had been fine, until now. Being back here made all the reasons why he had left here. It hit him like a ton of bricks that were knocking him down piece by wretched piece.

Cain, his military guard dog and officer in arms, was at his side. For the first time in years, Cain was on a lead. Military officer or not, Cain would have to stay on his lead for the duration of their stay here.

Surprisingly, Darryl thought as he looked down at Cain, his giant Riesen schnauzer, who was adjusting well to being on a lead, was more comfortable in his own skin then Darryl felt. Darryl shook the simple steel chain lead to get his attention. Cain looked up at him from his side panting and looked back over at the crowd in front of them, his thick black beard moving with him. His thick strong, black cropped, straight ears were standing at attention, and that was a good sign, Darryl told himself. Even Cain's stubby tail was wagging, Darryl noticed as he looked Cain over.

Darryl took an unsteady deep breath and looked back up at the crowd before him knowing his family was in for a surprise tonight and he was unsure if that excited him or not. His father, Quinn Krause, was the only person here who knew that Darryl was back stateside.

All he could do was hope and pray that after twelve years, everyone in this room had forgotten what he looked like so he could just stand here for a moment longer and take in his surroundings. He looked around and noticed then, that he didn't remember any of them.

Well, except maybe Coach Mike, he told himself with a smile, seeing his old high school football coach standing next to someone Darryl honestly didn't know. He couldn't forget the man he owed his thanks too for every time his knee and shoulder popped out of place. Coach Mike had pushed him hard toward victory during all those practices and games only to serve up the endurance he used now to fight in the military with, and the aches and pains in his joints he felt every time he pushed himself too hard, he thought with an awkward grin.

Darryl noticed his father Quinn talking to one of his family members toward the front of the room as he looked around Coach Mike to scan the crowd. A few days ago, Darryl had gotten the call from his father that had brought him here. Curtis Stone, Darryl's uncle, had passed away.

Darryl had left his station in Ireland immediately to be here with his family. He had just a few more days left on leave, and planned on spending them with his family, even though Luna Pier was the last place on the face of this earth that he wanted to be.

With a heavy grieving heart, he scanned the crowd next to his father looking for his mother. Aquila Stone Krause would be overjoyed to see her only son, but Darryl knew her heart was heavy tonight. Her younger brother Curtis had died in the line of service as a firefighter. Darryl had been thinking of her, and his family, ever since he got the call from his father to be here with her.

Darryl looked down at his uniform once more. His tie was straight, his boots were shiny, and his uniform was impressively clean and starched to perfection. He ran his hand through his tight military cut hair one last time. He knew she would only be proud of the man he had become and would care less how impressive he looked. All his loving mother would care about was that her son was home. He hoped it would relieve a little of the pain he knew she was experiencing tonight.

And with that last thought he stood a little a taller then and pulled on Cain's lead to do the same. They looked ready, albeit they didn't feel it, they did the best they both possibly could. They had dusted off the weight of their last assignment abroad and spent all day yesterday cleaning up so they could be here tonight with his family. Relaxed, refreshed, and somewhat mortal again.

Aquila's brothers, Darryl's uncles, were all firefighters, along with Darryl's grandfather, Frank Stone, and his father before him. Curtis was the oldest son of Frank's, and had been the assistant chief alongside Frank who was the chief of the Luna Pier Fire Department. Darryl knew a firefighter's death was hard on everyone involved. Tonight, it was going to be hard on all of them.

Darryl knew everyone in this building tonight he thought as he looked around some more and started to recognize some of the strange faces he was seeing. As Darryl looked around he noticed every emergency personnel from all around Monroe County were here tonight with his family. It was easy to tell their professions apart by the attire of their clothing. The firefighters were wearing their dress suit uniforms, the police offices were in their uniforms, and the paramedics were wearing their dress uniform shirts. On everyone's badges there was a black stripe ribbon across it in remembrance of their fallen brother, Curtis.

As much as Darryl hated to admit it, he was glad everyone he knew was in the same building, it would make saying goodbye easier in a few days.

The way Curtis had died though, Darryl shook his head looking down at his new black dress boots, was enough to make him want to turn and run from this place tonight. It brought memories back for him that he had spent years, and a lot of money trying to forget about. But duty, he thought as he stood taller, duty and honor to his family was all that was keeping him here. It was all that had made him fly back here.

He hadn't been back here since...

Darryl refused to think about it and instead looked around the crowd again looking for his mother as he held tighter onto Cain's lead like a lifeline. Cain looked up at him in confusion then, whimpering to let him know he was there. Darryl looked down at him and smiled, reassured Cain and shook his hand a little so the lead would loosen its hold on him.

Cain, Darryl thought as he looked back up to the crowd around him, had seen him through and gotten him out of every dangerous situation known to a soldier, but tonight Cain would just have to sit and stay by his side. They couldn't run from here.

As Darryl looked over the crowd, he refused to think of all the reasons why he hadn't come back here. He refused to get caught up in himself tonight. His family needed him, and he would do the right thing by them. Even if it was killing him to do it.

Darryl looked again for the third time. He hadn't really been looking before, but now he tried. When he found his mother, she was crying with Darryl's Aunt Isabella, his mother's youngest sister. He knew he was going to need a moment to himself before he could go to them. His fine, dutiful composer shattered in one split second seeing his mother cry.

Darryl looked around and noticed out the large picture window next to a discreet back door, that his Uncle Asher was outside leaning against a pillar. It was hard not to notice Asher. His height and build was much like Darryl's own; he also towered over a crowd like a sore thumb. But it was Asher's roguish blonde hair that was always a mess and his rugged 5 o'clock shadow that was some times out of place that gave him away. Darryl thought about his uncle and shook his head. Asher would never have met up to military standards very well. It was why the fire department suited him so well.

Darryl quietly walked over to the door and headed out to see him with Cain by his side. He hoped no one had noticed him yet. He headed toward the door behind the crowd. "I'm not a coward," he reminded himself; he was just a man who didn't want to be here.

"I'm not a coward Cain." He told his dog as he led him through the door. "I'm just not a damn fool either."

He thought to himself, thinking about what seeing his mother crying had done to him, and would have done to him if he would have walked over to her. It was as good excuse as any.

Pain could make even the strongest of men falter. Darryl refused to falter. He had seen the pain his mother was feeling while she held her little sister. It was a pain Darryl remembered all too well. Darryl could handle all kinds of pain that much he knew for sure. He just wasn't ready for the blow he knew would come feeling that pain again. The blow that would knock him off his feet and take him back twelve years in time.

Asher and Curtis had not only been his uncles, but his best friends as they all grew up in high school together. He looked up to the two of them growing up in high school. He admired the men they had become, and hoped he had impressed them with the man he had become.

Curtis wasn't much older than Darryl, he thought as he walked up to Asher. Only three years separated them. They had been close, just like brothers. But after the accident had happened so many years ago, a lifetime ago, Darryl had left for good. He had never missed his uncles as much as he did right now.

His Uncle Asher noticed when Darryl walked outside. Darryl greeted him with a nod and a half smile as Asher pushed off the pillar he had been leaning against and blew out his smoke he had just inhaled. Darryl then reached out his hand to Asher in greeting.

Asher straightened up when Darryl reached him and shook Darryl's hand. It was a sure and strong in a familiar manner. He returned to leaning against the pillar smoking.

With Cain sitting perched at his flank, Darryl introduced Cain to Asher and explained who he was as he reached in his dress pant pockets for his own smokes he desperately needed in that moment and lit up a smoke next to his uncle on the pillar across from him, taking up the same stance as he was watching their smoke billow out before them in the warm summer night.

Darryl needed this moment to regain his composer, and to see how Asher was doing. It was something they had all shared in the past; a smoke together, alone, lost in thought. The only thing that was missing was Curtis.

"How long are you home for?" Asher broke the silence first, flicking away some of his ashes of his smoke.

Asher asked him this, not really looking at him, Darryl noticed. Asher adjusted his foot that was resting on the pillar behind him as he took another hit of his own smoke and lifted his head skyward as he blew out a puff of smoke, resting his head there and closing his eyes in surrender.

"I have a few more days left here." Darryl said to him reassuringly. He knew his uncle would want to spend time with him now that he was here.

Darryl refused to acknowledge this place as home like Asher had asked. It wasn't home anymore, he thought as he dug his booted foot on the sidewalk and slid his free hand in one of his pockets that was holding onto Cain's steel lead.

"It took time to get here. I was called to Washington for a meeting once I got stateside, and I have to go back as soon as I'm done here."

Asher chuckled next to him. "Sometimes I think you are married to that damn Army, Darryl."

Darryl chuckled in reply as he took a hit of his smoke. He would never use the word married to describe his devotion to the military, but it made sense. Sometimes he felt he was just born this way. Serving was all he had ever wanted to do.

"Yeah. So how you holding up, man?" He asked Asher, trying to get the conversation off him.

He noticed Asher was looking up at the sky dodging his question though.

"Have you seen your mother yet?" Asher said to him after a long sigh while he blew out more smoke.

Darryl took note of that. Asher didn't want to talk about it, and that was fine with him. He hadn't really wanted to know anyhow, it was just common courtesy to ask. He knew Asher was a mess, whether he wanted to admit or not. His hair in the disarray it was in and his unshaven state spoke volumes as to how he felt. If it wasn't for his dress firefighter uniform he was wearing- well, then again, Darryl told himself, Asher could always pull off the rugged look better than most guys he knew, no matter what he was wearing.

"No, not yet." He said quietly, breathing in the last of his smoke to Asher's question. "I needed a moment."

Asher nodded in acknowledgment at Darryl's words. "It's a bad habit." He said smiling at his own smoke and cocking a half knowing smile toward Darryl.

Darryl smiled at that. It was Asher's way of not talking about serious things. Asher had said that to him every time they were together in high school smoking. It had been Asher's duty as Darryl's uncle to say at least that. But Asher never judged him for it.

Darryl flicked out his smoke and held out his fist for Asher to bump when they caught each other's eyes knowingly. When Asher returned it, Asher grabbed Darryl's hand pulling him in for an awkward hug and thumped Darryl on the back. "Ah! It's good to see you again Darryl."

Darryl nodded to him. "It's good to see you too Asher."

"Uncle." Asher reminded him squeezing his hand in a manly jester.

The rebuke was lost on Darryl this time unlike when they were growing up. They weren't boys anymore.

Darryl stood taller in front of Asher then and put on his best smile after he had eyed Asher intently. He hadn't meant to feel Asher's jester as a threat, but it was what he was trained to do. Even Cain noticed the exchange. Darryl was not only a grown man of thirty-one years, but he was a destructive force to be reckoned with in his world. He made sure Asher felt it in his hand shake and embrace that though Asher might be Darryl's uncle, Darryl had fully grown into a man none of them had ever dreamed he would.

Darryl left Asher there with his thoughts and a firm handshake and then he walked back into the parlor of the funeral home. Asher was out here for a reason Darryl knew all too well, and he wanted to leave him to his peace.

Plus, he thought with a sigh as he headed back to the door, he needed to find his mother.

As he opened the door, a young woman passed him. He had to hold Cain back with a forceful command as she did. Cain had been taken off guard by the woman who was walking outside and Darryl was sure that was the only reason Cain had lunged towards her and growled.

Well, he hoped that was all the reason why. Cain was trained in the military to protect Darryl from danger and any enemy. Darryl looked at the woman who had passed him and then back at Cain who was staring her down in a posture that clearly said he was unsure of her.

She was stunningly beautiful when she smiled at him and thanked him for holding open the door Darryl noticed, she even politely smiled at Cain even though he was growling at her. He watched as she moved to Asher's side in wonder. She was dressed in a silk black dress with splashes of color outlining irises. Her long brown curled hair swirled around her slim form in waves that moved sensually with her body. She was tiny in stature, but she moved and carried herself with a grace that excelled most women these days.

And her smile, Darryl wondered about her smile as she reached Asher, it was so… real. He could have sworn he had never seen so real of a smile before.

Darryl smiled over at Asher then. Asher had finally found himself someone. Darryl was honestly happy for him as he watched their hands intertwine. Darryl was a little astounded by Asher's choice. She was awfully small for Asher, but he would tease him for that later. Whoever she was, she was sure to make Asher a happy man indeed.

Cain on the other hand, wasn't. He growled at attention toward the woman, and Darryl had to pull him back through the door just to get his mind off the woman.

"Not today Cain." He told him, as they walked together into the parlor. "Today we are off duty. Today, here, you and I can both relax." He said more to himself than to Cain as he looked back over the crowd. They would worry about the war they were in once they got back to work. "Understand?" He asked Cain, as he looked back around and noticed no one was paying attention to either of them.

When Cain finally sat next to him and huffed through his beard after he had looked back at the door one last time, Darryl knew he was over it. "Let's go." He told Cain as they walked forward together.

He walked up to the front of the room where his mother and father were standing and noticed pictures of Curtis. He stopped briefly and looked, longingly at them for a moment. Cain sat down immediately with another huff and Darryl noticed. He smiled and tried to ignore Cain. He got lost in thoughts of Curtis as he looked at the pictures on the board in front of him and let his mind go back to the times they had spent together.

Curtis and Asher had played sports together in high school with Darryl at Luna Pier High School. Memories Darryl hadn't thought about in what felt like forever flooded his mind. Pictures of the three of them dressed in full football gear together after a game, and pictures of them at graduation were on the board. He had forgotten all about these pictures, he thought, as he reached out and touched one with his fingers.

One picture, though, took him off guard and the unwanted treacherous emotions he had been dreading for days welled up inside of him. The blow he hadn't anticipated yet hit him like a bomb being dropped next to him.

Cain nudged his moist nose into Darryl's hand just as he had taken a deep relaxing breath. Cain whined and wanted his attention. Cain didn't understand his commander's change in emotions.

Memories of the woman standing in the picture with him, Curtis and Asher started to enter his mind. The only reason she wasn't in the graduations pictures with him and his uncles was because she never made it to graduation.

Darryl's Post Traumatic Stress Disorder or whatever his military doctors had called it, made him look away and cuss out loud as it kicked into full gear and he tried to down shift it. He heard the intake of breath from the couple behind him at his colorful use of curse words, and he ignored the two completely. As ungentlemanly as it was, he had other things to worry about. When he finally got his composure back he looked back at the board of pictures.

Chills. A fevered rush coursed through every vein in his body, pumping heated blood all throughout him. Ice cold sweat broke out on his heated temple. And then, that tingling sensation started. It started at his fingers, and then ran up his wrist to his forearm. Darryl had to close his eyes at the memory of the woman who used to touch his fingers, and then run her fingers up his hand past his wrist to his forearm, in just the same manner.

Darryl opened his eyes then and looked drunkenly at the woman in the picture who he had wrapped in his arms. The woman in his memories had faded with time, but the picture in front of him brought her image back to life. Her eyes were closed in his embrace in the picture he had never seen before but remembered posing for. Asher and Curtis next to them were oblivious to the moment that she and he were sharing together. Darryl remembered that moment time had stood still for. He pulled the picture free from the pins and looked closer at her.

Just as he was about to breath her name in a whisper he hadn't done in twelve years his mother spotted him and called out his name in surprise. He closed his eyes then and tried to forget about the woman in the picture as he tucked it quietly in his dress pant pocket.

Not tonight, not here, he reminded himself turning at the sound of his mother's voice, just as Cain did and headed over to her. The woman in picture, the woman in his memory, the reasons why he hated coming back here, all forgotten at the sound of his mother's grieving voice.

With a staying command to Cain, he wrapped her in his arms and held her while she softly cried. She was unhappy for the reasons he was here, but happy all the same.

Darryl knew he owed his mother this moment as he held her. He gave it to her freely as he held her while she wept in his chest. He knew right then in that moment that her grief was his fault. He had been gone from her for too long.

His father came to him next, and gave him the same awkward hug Asher had given him. It was what men did. The only time they did it.

His grandmother was next; and so on it went as he greeted his family one by one, introducing them to Cain when needed. He was proud of Cain in those moments. He was doing well tonight, and Darryl was thankful he was with him. Grateful, that at any given notice, Cain would lead him away from this place as fast as they could go, like they had done so many times in the past together when they were trapped.

When it was time for them all to be seated, he sat next to his father. He listened and watched as the funeral for his uncle began and was hauntingly painful for him.

Memories and emotions he didn't want to see or feel haunted him to the point Cain noticed.

Darryl had been here before. Years ago, in this same building, he tried not to think about it, but he couldn't help it. Everything was so painfully the same as it had been before.

The same people were here in the same building. Everyone was older now, but Darryl still felt the child he had been then. After all these years and he still couldn't help it. He still couldn't fight it.

Darryl closed his eyes and as he rested his elbow on his knee he pinched his nose as memories he couldn't hinder any longer played out for him in his mind abidingly.

Cain laid his head on Darryl's leg and Darryl reached down to place his other hand on Cain's head blindly. He couldn't look at anyone, not even Cain. He needed a moment.

The woman in the picture hidden in his pocket, Talia Rose Kruse, had given her life just like Curtis had done, just like the men were praising Curtis for in their message.

But she had it done for Darryl. She had been praised as a hero even though Darryl had hated them for it. She had died, and Darryl would have freely given his own life to save her from the death that had taken her from him.

Her brother, Ken Kruse, the fire departments Chaplin, was now preaching the same message he had given at his little sister's funeral, and it was tearing Darryl in pieces. She had paid a price no woman ever should have to pay. She had saved his life in the car accident. She had been so badly burned trying to save Darryl's life, that she had lost her own life.

Curtis was being praised now as a hero. Just like they all had praised Talia.

Darryl looked up through squinted eyes and looked around. He couldn't do this here. If he was going to fall, he damn sure wasn't going to do it in front his family.

"Dad, I-" Darryl said to his father trying to excuse himself.

"It's ok. I know. Go." His father said to him with a nod and smile of assurance.

Darryl stood then and excused himself taking Cain with him.

When the firemen started lining up to salute Curtis who was no longer alive, and his family, Darryl was glad he was at the back of the room and couldn't see the services anymore. Asher would be walking up next to talk, and Darryl couldn't handle that either. It would be too hard to watch Asher fall to pieces.

Death was too hard to see. Grieving was worse. He needed to find strength and he wasn't going to find it here.

Darryl stood in the men's room looking into the mirror at the man he had become. He wasn't the boy in those pictures anymore. He was more than just a man now also. He was a soldier.

A killer.

The thought made him look away from the mirror, not really wanting to look at himself anymore.

Darryl had learned early on when joining the intelligence agency of the Army that there were enemies in this world worse than ever seen before. Darryl was recruited to hunt these men down and kill them. To know the enemy inside and out. To never lose sight of his mission or his enemy. Being a hunter and a killer had changed who he had been since he had left here twelve years ago, but his mind and his heart had never forgotten who he had once been. Being in the Army had only distracted him from the events that happened here.

The last time he had been here, Curtis had been alive, and they were not the men they were now. They were young and innocent then. Their lives had been touched by death and fire then, and it had hurt them then just as much as it was hurting Darryl now.

He hung his head willing the memories of Talia to fade.

But they wouldn't.

He couldn't think of Curtis or his family without seeing her face there too with them. She had been that much a part of his life back then that his family had been her family.

He could see her laughing as her long blonde hair danced around her shoulders. Her smile had been what he had lived for then. Now, now as he looked inside the mirror at the man who stood before him he had become, he didn't know what he lived for anymore.

Darryl looked down at his hands that were resting on the sink. He could hear his military doctor telling him that this was a very bad idea and had to chuckle at himself. This was always a bad idea, but no one understood how it felt, how he longed to think of her, to just remember her for one moment. And at times when he finally broke down and did it, he could swear he could feel her again. Chills would run down him, and he could feel the brush of her hand on him. He couldn't understand it, he couldn't explain it, but he could feel it. It would so easily do things to him that would drive him madly insane with desire and the pleasure it caused inside him was addicting even though it was so hauntingly painful to forget about.

Cain had inched closer to him in a soft bark, grabbing his hand and gnawing on it gently begging him to stop as the tears fell down Darryl's face in remembrance of all the things that had haunted him these past years. He could see the tears that had started to flow down his cheeks falling on his hands. He brushed them away harshly.

And then, like magic, it happened. Thoughts of her, memories he had long forgotten, came rolling back into his mind like gentle waves on a shore.

Talia had been his best friend growing up. The thought gave Darryl chills down his spine. It had been so long since he had let thoughts of her back in his mind. He had to shake off the chill so he could think.

It had been odd for him to call her that. She wasn't a guy, and their friends had teased them both about being so close. But he hadn't cared. That's what she had been. His best friend.

Darryl let other memories flow through his mind. He knew he shouldn't, and knew he was going to pay for it later, but he had to if he was ever going to get out of this men's room alive.

Darryl had met Talia on his first day of school in kindergarten on the bus. Scared of his own height, which was taller than most boys his age, and his deep blue eyes his mother loved, but others had said were a 'scary' blue color, Darryl had set himself up for a day of disappointment at school that day. But it was Talia, who had commented on his eyes that were the exact same color as hers that had put his childish fears to rest. She had loved him at first sight. And he had fallen in love with her all that very first day.

When he had boarded the bus that day headed for Luna Pier Elementary school, the bus driver, Talia's mother Helen, had greeted him, zipped up his jacket he had forgotten to do on his own and told him since it was his first day that he could sit with her daughter Talia. It was her first day also.

Darryl had walked past her mother the and found himself sitting next to an angel. Talia's smile and long blonde hair had been breathtaking to him. She had showed him her pretty necklace and bracelet she was wearing, and had asked him if her hair had looked okay. Darryl had told her she was beautiful, and with the real, honest smile that formed on her lips, making her cheeks blush, Darryl realized at the age of 5, he was head over heels in love with her. And he was still in love with her to this day.

They had shared the same class together that day, and because her last name was spelled almost like his, give or take a letter, they had shared the closeness that one simple coincidence had given them all throughout their school days. They kept their lockers close together all throughout school and their hands closer. Every time he turned around she was next to him. And he hadn't cared one bit.

Summers, vacations, weekends; whenever they were out of school they could be found playing together. She wasn't much of a base runner back then, but she sure as hell could throw a curveball better than any of his friends, and she always made sure the ball found its way to his glove instead of his friends. Just like she did with her heart.

Mud and dirt didn't bother her as much as it did her mother, and he had to admit she looked better all dressed up than she did in ripped up holy jeans and a ponytail, but as hard as he ever did try, she never liked getting dressed up. It suited him just fine most days. She ran faster in jeans then she did in a dress, and as he got older it didn't matter what she was wearing, he was still heartbreakingly in love with her.

He had taught her to ride a bike, and she had taught him how to read. He taught her to fish, and she had taught him how to swim. She taught him how to read and quote Shakespeare word for word along with every other poetry book she could find, and he taught her how to sing all the sweetest love songs he and Asher could play on the guitar.

Darryl couldn't think of those days that had gone by too fast anymore. They would only lead him up to the last days with her. He refused to think about them here.

He looked back into his past one last time. He thought of the last time he had kissed her. The reaction in his body caused his heart to race. A few weeks before their graduation, he had been on the beach with her, wrapped up behind her sitting on the rocks, with the ring she had always wanted to be hers in his hand, asking her to spend the rest of their lives together after high school. He couldn't graduate without knowing for sure they would spend the rest of their lives together. The military wasn't much of a life for a wife, but he was sure she would have been the best one for the job.

When she had said yes, Darryl had kissed her like never before. It was the last time he ever did, he thought lowering his head. It was the only kiss he could still feel on his lips when he thought about her.

Darryl walked back out to his family and tried to plaster on a fake smile for them as Cain greeted them before he could. They all would see the redness there in his eyes. They all would know what his heart had gone through this night being here again. He hadn't only lost Curtis, but he had lost Talia all over again.

His mother knew, but she never said anything. She only touched his shoulder a time or two with a knowing smile he knew was all she could give him in those moments. As they all walked out toward the front doors, Darryl grabbed his bag he had left by the doors. He turned and looked for Asher to tell him he wanted to stay at his house while he was here. He couldn't see his old house where he had spent years loving Talia yet, not tonight he told himself. He wouldn't be able to sleep in his room and look out his window where her face had been pressed up against the glass on countless days and nights to see if he wanted to come outside and play. Her ghost would haunt him there and he wasn't ready for that again.

As Darryl looked around for his uncle and spotted him, he could see the way Asher was looking at the woman he had seen him with earlier. She was smiling at him from where she was standing by the doors where Darryl was.

Asher knew what love was now. He could see it in his eyes. Darryl watched as she turned gracefully and left the parlor followed by her own family.

Darryl explained to his mother where he would be staying when she kissed him goodbye, but he had to tug on Cain to sit. Cain was still growling at Asher's girlfriend who had just left. He started to tug on the lead and looked back at Darryl confused and then back at the door whining.

"I'm sorry mom; he must need to go outside." He said softly apologizing to his mother as he looked down at Cain and scolded him.

Darryl noticed immediately that the hair on Cain's back was standing up and he was silently growing inside himself. He whimpered and looked back at Darryl again.

Immediately, the hair on Darryl's own hair back stood as they locked eye contact. All of his years of training kicked into full drive. He followed Cain's gaze. Cain was looking at the family of Asher's girlfriend like he did their enemy. Cain had responded to her the same way he was now when she had passed them by earlier.

It couldn't be... he wondered to himself. Cain was trained to seek and find the enemy for Darryl. Could her family be...?

He looked sharply down at Cain and tugged on his lead. He wanted to say no to Cain, but something was gnawing at the back of his mind. Asher's girlfriend couldn't have been a-

"I love you sweetheart." His mother told him interrupting his thoughts, squeezing his hand and pulling him out of his own head. She softly patted Cain's head. "I'll see you two soon." She smiled with tear filled eyes, completely oblivious of what had just happened between the two, and turned to walk outside with Darryl's father.

Darryl took one last look at the family Cain had noticed as they got in their cars and left, he turned and watched as Asher had all but pushed the crowd out of his way just to make it to the doors before her and her family had left. For whatever reason the woman and her family had left without saying goodbye and Asher was awestruck by it.

Seeing the look of defeat and the frightening look on Asher's face, Darryl thought better of questioning him. But the years spent together with Cain in training and in war, Cain had never led him astray. Darryl looked down at Cain and studied his posture. Cain was eager and ready and thoroughly befuddled by Darryl's actions.

"Come on Cain. It's not what you're thinking it is." He told Cain as he walked him over to Asher.

They were off duty. Cain just needed to get used to that. This enemy they had been fighting for years abroad had never made to their home land.

Or had it...

Darryl left with Asher, and was headed to Asher's house where Darryl and Cain would stay while he was here in Luna Pier. He left Asher alone to his own thoughts the best he could on the way home. He could tell Asher was hurting. They talked about high school, mentioning Curtis at times, but always avoiding the subject when they could. Asher was kind enough to never mention Talia, Darryl noticed.

"Remember that day we flipped my old truck that winter in the ditch on Luna Pier Road?" Darryl questioned him.

Asher laughed out loud blowing smoke out his window. "We were all hanging by our seat belts daring each other who would let go first."

Neither one spoke again for a while. They both remembered who had gone first. Talia had.

"That's when I had to buy my SUV." Darryl said in almost a whisper blowing out his own smoke out his window. "She loved that damn SUV."

But Asher heard him and took note of it. Darryl still missed her, Asher thought to himself.

When they parked in Asher's drive, Asher showed him inside his cap cod bachelor pad that was right on the pier and left once Darryl and Cain got settled. Asher needed to be alone and Darryl understood that.

Asher's little dog Cookie, did not like that he and Cain were in her home, and barked at them throughout every room they went into.

After he took off his dress coat and laid it on Asher's couch he undid his tie and unbuttoned his shirt. Looking around at Asher's house, Darryl was impressed. Asher had remodeled the house nicely. He had added a touch of firefighting d cor to every room. From glass coffee tables held up by fire hydrants, to the sink faucets that looked like the end of a hose nozzle on the trucks, and the fire fighter helmets hanging over his pool table in his dining room that lit up the table. Asher had pictures of sports and fire trucks hanging on his walls, and shelves that held past awards he had earned during his service on the fire department.

What really caught Darryl's eye, was the small mini bar shelves that lined Asher's counter in the kitchen. It was unique for a house to have, with the mirror wall behind it looking just like what you would find in a bar. He even had beer dispenser pulls in front of the seating area. Darryl was impressed. Asher's kitchen was everything every guy had ever dreamed of for a kitchen. There was even a flat screen television hanging on the wall. His stove, in the center of the room, even had a gas grill top for grilling up meat. The ovens on the adjacent wall were made of three different sizes. Perfect for any man who knew how to use them.

"I never knew Asher could cook." He said to Cain who looked up at him.

Darryl walked out and sat out on Asher's front porch with Cain by his side, who was no longer on his steel lead. He basically did it for Cookie, who was so annoyed by their presence. She had went upstairs to Asher's room to pout and be alone, even though she continued to bark at them from the top of the stairs.

Darryl was dressed in only a white t-shirt and jeans and let the night surround him as he let the memories of Talia flood his mind again. Asher had very comfortable lounge chairs out there where Darryl could prop up his feet on the ledge and stare off on the moon lit water of Lake Erie in front of him. It was peaceful with only the sounds of the summer breeze mixed with crashing waves on the shore to distract him.

Hours later he watched the swirl of sweet whiskey turn in a glass he had poured for himself out of Asher's stash in his kitchen. He was grateful Asher had enough of it and smokes to last him a few days here. He was going to need it. He stared off over the moon sparkling Lake Erie toward the unmistakable lighthouse off in the distance. He had missed nights like this on the pier. The soft warm summer breeze gently stirred in his military cut black hair. He rubbed his head and watched as Cain slept peacefully for the first time in years on Asher's front porch.

He had done this often on nights like this in Ireland. Nights when he wasn't on duty and his men had left him alone. When duty didn't call him and he could just stop thinking.

The night of the accident had happened almost exactly twelve years ago. He and Talia had gotten in his SUV they had parked by the beach just a few blocks down from where he was now after he had proposed to her. He had dropped her off at her house and had foolishly sped down her drive back home at a speed that was dangerous in this small town, excited to tell his own family the news.

Darryl closed his eyes tightly and took a long gulp of the whiskey in his hand as he remembered how he had been hit by an unknown driver when he had turned onto Harold Road. He assumed it was a drunk driver; they would never find the person or the car, head on. Darryl had been knocked unconscious during the crash.

Somehow, Talia had come to his rescue, but his SUV had started on fire with her in it. He had woken up to her screams on the paved road where she had pushed him out of the SUV. But he couldn't get to her in time. He had injured his back in the crash, and the pain of it hindered his efforts getting to her. By the time he had gotten to her, it had been too late. He had held her burnt body in his arms until his grandfather and uncles on the fire department had come to their rescue.

Darryl rubbed his head with his cold glass. He still didn't understand what had happened. He had never regained his memories of the crash. Only the moments before when he had been with her, and then her screams that had awakened him. It was all he could remember.

He could still hear them.

She had never screamed like that in their whole lives.

He would never forget them.

He looked at his arm then. There was still a patch there that ran up his hand to his arm of burnt flesh. It matched the one on his chest. It would never heal, it would never go away. It was a constant reminder of where he had held her for too long, where the back of her burnt head had rested on his arm.

Darryl gulped down what was left of his drink and squeezed his eyes shut tight then. For a brief moment, he could see through his young eyes her burnt body. It haunted him still.

When the scent hit him, the memory of the smell of the fire mixed with her flesh, he got up and walked down the porch steps. He guessed Asher had the right idea tonight. He was going to walk this night out of him tonight, and forget about it all. He had too.

Cain was right at his side, loyal dog that he was.

Chapter Two: Here

The next few days, Darryl spent with his family, and alone.

He took out Asher's motorcycle and rode around Luna Pier absentmindedly finding all the places he had spent with Talia. No matter where he went in this damn city, it reminded him of her.

The beach house, the bowling alley, the movie theater, and all their favorite restaurants; they were all reminders of places they had been together. The private beach off Menders bend where he had spent time tanning and laying with her during the summer days, just reading and singing together. The roads in Luna Pier they had walked down holding hands daydreaming about their future together and their past. The high school, the middle school, even Luna Pier elementary school where they had spent their first years together. So many years, so many cherished moments he would never forget about.

The bike reminded him of the one he had owned with her behind him all those years ago. Her arms around his waist haunted his mind and made it hard for him to steer. The way she had looked in the mirrors behind him, like the world around them did not exist any longer. The way her hands would hold onto his sides and the way he could feel her behind him pressed up against him.

Darryl would give anything to go back to that last day and do it over again so differently. He shook his head thinking out loud, "Damn right." As he put one hand on his thigh, he tried not to look at the road because the wind only made his tears fall harder.

This is why he never came back here, he reminded himself. This is why he had spent so many years abroad, he told himself harshly brushing away his treacherous tears. Why he spent so many years serving and fighting for his country. It was out of duty, yes, but also out of self-preservation. The farther away he got from here, the farther he got away from her.

When he came into Luna Pier, he had to hold onto the bike where he had stopped in front of the gates of the cemetery where Talia was buried. He looked hauntingly at where her grave was. The head stone that read her name he could see in his mind even though he wasn't standing in front of it.

He lowered his head at memories of his younger self sitting in front of her head stone, cursing God for taking her from him. He had pulled out grass and Earth then and had thrown it toward the heavens knowing damn well he couldn't dig her out of the grave and bring her back to life then.

Taking a deep breath, he rocked the motorcycle to the side as he stepped on the kickstand and lowered it to the ground. He walked the length of two hundred feet slowly to her grave. The shaking started as the tears fell drunkenly from his eyes seeing her name on the head stone again. Her name blurred in his teary eyes. He looked heaven ward again toward the clouds that hung over the lake. He still didn't understand God's reasons for taking her.

"It should be me here. Not her." He prayed as he looked at her head stone shaking his head.

He wiped his tears and stuffed his hands in his pockets trying to control his breathing. He never got the answers he needed from God, now wasn't any different than before.

He tried not to think about her body that lay under his feet. If he did, he would dig the six feet down with his bare hands just to touch her one last time.

Within seconds, a feeling came rushing over him. An old feeling he remembered he had felt the last time he had been here just days after they had laid her to rest. It was a feeling he got every now and again, and every time he felt it, it scared the hell out of him.

He could feel her. He didn't know how or why, but he could feel her.

With a deep breath, he closed his eyes and sighed greatly gulping down the tear water that was pooling in his mouth. "I'll never forget you Talia.

"I promise." He told her as he walked away and drove back into the Pier.

Darryl spent time at Curtis' house saying goodbye to him with Asher as they packed up Curtis' things and discussed putting his house up for sale. He spent time with his mother and his grandmother Cyndy who were cleaning Curtis' house trying to understand why Curtis had to die too. He didn't have any answers for them, but he listened to them as they mourned.

He ran into Ken Kruse on his way into the fire hall the day before his last day was up. He stopped at the fire hall to see if the guys needed a hand on a call, but they were just getting back to the station when Darryl walked up. Ken was the one person Darryl wasn't looking forward to talking too, but something was telling him he needed too.

He walked around the old fire hall still mystified by the smell of fire and smoke he had forgotten about over the years. He wondered how Asher's own house smelled just like it. But then again, his grandparent's house had always smelled like this too.

Darryl was dressed in a dark blue Army t-shirt, a pair of combat boots, and jeans. He looked just like the men around him, except for his military persona and his dog tags that hung on his chest.

He talked to his uncles, Jesse and James, and once he was alone with Jerry, an old friend who was now the chief of police, he listened in on Jerry's conversation with Ken.

There were things going on in the world around these men that Darryl was not allowed to tell them about. Things he could only hope hadn't reached their home land yet. He found himself eager to make sure.

He had spent so much time here in this city he had forgotten what all was happening around the world. But that was why he was here, right? To forget about work so he could grieve.

It was Jerry's words that brought him back to reality like a slap in the face he wasn't ready for.

"Those rioters in the news are not terrorist Ken. All of the departments are talking about it. They're some kind of-"

Jerry looked at Darryl then after he saw the expression Darryl made at his last comment. He could tell Darryl knew something about the rumors going on around the world. US citizens were angry and police officers like himself were losing the battle to rioters and looters who were protesting about the involvement the US was not taking in the matter.

"Some places are like a war zones Ken. It hasn't hit the Pier yet though, but it will if Detroit or Toledo is hit by the riots."

"Any word on how the government is going to handle all this Darryl?"

So it had hit their home land already, Darryl thought to himself. Jerry was right. The rioters and looters Jerry was talking about wasn't what it seemed. In other countries, it had been the enemy's way of destroying towns and cities first, then taking them down and killing everyone in them leaving officials mystified by how it had happened.

Everyone here was planning for something they didn't know how to plan for, Jerry told him. All of the emergency personnel in Monroe County were worried. What were they to do if it hit home?

Darryl wished he could tell them even their government here wouldn't know what to do. He was their only saving grace and here he was taking a 'break' from it all, then he would be leaving them all here defenseless. But he thought better of telling Jerry as he looked down at his boots and shoved his hands in his pockets. There were some things he was bound by not to speak of. Even to family. All he could do was take this knowledge with him to Washington and hope they had a plan.

Ken came to his rescue before he had to say anything at all.

"He's an Army Intel commander Jerry. He knows things even the government doesn't know. I'm sure he's not allowed to tell you either." Ken took a second to look at Darryl and winked at him. Then turned back to Jerry. "Plus he's home now, last thing he wants to do is talk about work."

Ken thumped Darryl on the back and wrapped his arm around Darryl's neck in a gesture that Darryl remembered.

Jerry had let Darryl off the hook thanks to Ken, and Darryl was thankful for it. Jerry shook his hand and apologized to him. "It was good to see you again, man. Come home and visit more often," Jerry said with a smile and a goodbye.

Darryl nodded and smiled back, but made no promise in coming back here.

"Hey Darryl, what's up man?" Ken asked, bumping his fist with Darryl as Jerry took his leave and got in his police cruiser.

"Not much man, how are you?" Darryl said with a smile.

Ken shrugged his shoulders. "As good as can be expected. How long are you home for?"

Darryl hated this question. This place wasn't home. He hated how it was starting to feel like it again. He looked down at the ground and tried to hide his dark mood. When he looked back up to Ken he took a deep breath and gave him his best smile and told him "Not much longer. I have a meeting in a few days in Washington."

And then like everyone else had done to him before he could explain the importance of why he was going there and why he wanted to see everyone one last time, he was interrupted.

Ken shook his head at Darryl. "I swear you are married to the Army man."

Darryl looked at him dumbfounded; Asher had said the same thing to him. There was so much more he wanted to say to Ken about that matter, but now wasn't the time.

"I heard you married Miranda?" Darryl said to Ken in a tone he hoped didn't reflect his mood, trying to change the subject.

Ken smiled and nodded bashfully. He told Darryl all about the wedding and the children they had together, as they turned and headed out the bay doors.

Darryl was very happy for them both.

Ken talked about the weather, and talked about the department. As they walked out to the pier by the beach he talked about home. Darryl tried to tell Ken about Ireland, but Ken always switched the conversation back to Luna Pier with a knowing smile.

Darryl didn't understand why everyone wanted him home- here, he corrected himself. Here. But it made him feel wanted, and he hadn't felt like that in a long time.

Not since- Darryl stopped himself before he thought about her again. But then, he realized who he was with, and another thought entered his mind.

A question he had been asking himself for long time, he knew only Ken could answer for him.

"Ken, you're a God man, can I ask you a question about Him?" Darryl asked as he shoved his hands in his pocket. They had rounded the first turn out on the pier, before they came to the end of the walk. He had been troubled about something ever since he'd gotten home- here. Here, he reminded himself again shaking his head. And he knew Ken was the man for the job.

Ken looked forward to this question every time he was asked. It was his job. His duty. His calling. He was the Chaplin on the department, and unlike his work as a firefighter, this was his chance to fight the hell fires, and he looked forward to them just as much as the earthly ones.

He looked over at Darryl then. "Of course. Anything. What's on your mind?"

"How does God choose who lives and who dies?" Darryl asked as he placed his arms and a booted foot on the pier rails in front of them and folded his hands together, looking out over the sunny, sparkling water of Lake Erie. "Why does he let the good ones go?" This last he said quietly lowering his head, truly and honestly not understanding the question.

He needed answers to that haunting question. He trusted no one else with them.

Like a life song singing out to him, Ken could hear the answers to that one question. He knew in his heart what Darryl was asking. Darryl wasn't asking about Curtis, he was asking about Talia.

Ken had just talked to Asher about the same thing like this not too long ago. Asher had wanted to know how he was supposed to know if he was in love with Emie Whitby or not. Ken knew now that even the strongest of men, when faced with love; fell hard enough to make them ask why.

Darryl had been in love with Talia, and even though she had been Ken's little sister, Ken hadn't cared. Darryl was the right man for her, and he had always wished them well together. But when she had died, while Ken and his family had rejoiced in her going to heaven, Darryl had been broken to pieces over losing her.

Ken had never known that all these years Darryl had questioned God's purposes in the matter. He wished now he had talked to him about it a long time ago. But Ken knew God worked in ways he would never be able to understand and with that Ken knew he needed this time with Darryl.

Ken followed Darryl's lead and took up a stance next to him.

"God doesn't pick and choose Darryl. There is a reason for everything."

Darryl didn't like that answer. His mother had said this to him the night Talia died. He looked at Ken sideways and said, "You can't tell me He wanted this. That He wanted her to die like that!"

Darryl hung his head then. He hadn't wanted Ken to know what he was thinking. He didn't want anyone to know he still thought of her, and how it tore him apart inside. "That He wanted Curtis to die like that." He said trying to sound like he was grieving over Curtis and not Talia who had died so long ago.

His questions grieved Ken. "Darryl, listen man. God's not like that. He didn't create us to kill us or destroy us." Ken laughed then to lighten the mood. "He's not some god sitting up there on a throne with a remote controller playing a game.

"God created us for a purpose. His reasons. Not ours. Believing in Him and that everything happens for a reason just isn't enough. It's learning to live that way, and to accommodate it when it happens, that changes your life. It's taking the gift of faith that is there for you to have and accepting it, applying it to your life the moment it happens, because in that moment that you forget that, you could miss out on so much man. We have to learn to trust Him, and stop blaming Him for things He didn't do."

"There is a reason for everything Darryl, even death. We won't know why until He reveals it to us."

Ken let that sit with him for a moment and prayed the seed he had planted would take root.

Darryl thought about Ken's words. That was the one thing he hadn't done yet. The one thing he couldn't do. He couldn't trust God with the reasons why. Darryl wouldn't like the answers. He'd always just blamed Him. And it made him feel better having someone to blame. He would never understand why God had let Talia die in the fire instead of him. And because there was no one else to blame for it, he blamed God.

Darryl knew if he ever found the man who had caused the accident he would strangle the life out of him.

He looked back over at Ken then. They shared a moment of silence as they looked over the lake.

"God says he will give you whatever you ask for Darryl. Just ask him for the answers. The reasons why."

"I don't want reasons. I don't want answers. I just want her." And for the first time he didn't care if anyone knew he still felt that way after all this time.

Ken had to leave the moment his wife Miranda called and Darryl envied him as he watched him leave.

Darryl spent his last day running. He ran on the beach in the early morning hours until the sun made him sweat and the sharp sand made his feet hurt. He cooled off and swam as far as his arms would let him out in the lake. When his body was weary and he was spent from pushing himself so hard; he sat on the rocks that lined the pier walls and watched the sail boats out in distance.

He couldn't trust his own thoughts anymore so he drowned them out with loud music blaring through the headphones of his work tablet he had attached to his arm. It helped. A little. Nagging thoughts of where he would be back to in a few days bothered him more than his thoughts of being here.

Later that day as the sun was setting, he knew his family was all gathered at his grandparents house, where he should be, but Darryl didn't want to be there just yet. His eyes were filled with unshed tears as he stood in front of his childhood home he somehow had walked to unintentionally with Cain waiting patiently by his side. He looked at the window of his old bedroom from the street. He could see Talia there haunting him again; up on her tiptoes looking in his window as her long blonde hair covered her young back.

Inside his room there he knew what was waiting for him. A lifetime of memories. He took a deep, shaky breath and looked down at Cain.

"Go see." It was a command, one Cain knew.

Cain ran softly up to the house and smelled, searched the grounds of Darryl's front lawn. When he made it to the front door and sniffed under the door inside, he turned and looked back at Darryl with a bark and sat patiently. It was safe.

Darryl smiled at him. He hadn't given the command for protection. He wouldn't need it here. He did it playfully for Cain. They would be back to work tomorrow and he didn't want Cain to get too lazy.

He looked down and stuffed his hands in his pockets as he walked up the front steps. He begged with whoever was listening in his heart to keep the overwhelming emotions that were threatening to overtake his will to wait until he was in the sanctuary of his room. He reached for the handle of the front door and took a second before he turned it, praying his mother had left it unlocked. When he turned the handle, he smiled. No one ever locked their doors in the Pier, he thought gratefully.

Cain followed him through the open front door and searched around his home protecting Darryl from danger as Darryl looked around. His mother had changed the d cor, but it was still home. And it still hurt to be here though, he thought, as he leaned up against the doorway to the living room and seen all his childhood pictures along with his military pictures he had sent back here for her display above the fireplace.

By the time Darryl found his room and found Cain waiting patiently in there for him, he leaned against the door post and just looked. He may be a thirty-year-old grown man, but his room made him feel like the child he had been.

Darryl sat on his bed as Cain sat dutifully next to him. He looked at the pictures that hung on his wall. Army trucks, guns and Stars lined his walls in posters that resembled the tattoos he now wore on his arms. His desk, which his eyes refused to look at, was just the way he had left it.

He closed his eyes and hung his head running his hands through hair. He could see the desk without even looking at it. A mirror, as tall as he was now, stood behind a computer screen that was too big for his desk. He smiled at that knowing the size of the tablet pc he used now did so much more than his huge old pc ever had.

Plastered all over the wall behind and around his desk were pictures and mementos of his childhood. Army brochures that were as worn out as his old baseball cards and a pair of fake dog tags he had made as a child hung from the mirror side.

He looked up then and looked at the mementos. It was the pictures of Talia that made him look down at his knees again. They were the pictures he had been running from his whole adult life. He couldn't even look at them even though he knew the images by heart. Nothing in that room mattered to him, he thought as he put his head in his hands. Nothing mattered anymore.

Except her, something whispered to his heart.

Darryl, from somewhere in the back of his heart, could hear her voice. Hear her calling to him. Her whisper was like the wind on his neck. It did things to him.

That feeling came over him again. That feeling he could feel in his soul. She was here again, haunting him.

Darryl opened his eyes then. He was no longer safe in his own head anymore. If she wasn't haunting his mind with images through his eyes, she was haunting his mind with her voice.

He looked up and walked over to the desk followed by Cain to her pictures. Darryl smiled down at Cain then. "Her name was Talia." Darryl told him. It was the first time he had ever talked to Cain about her. He had to wonder why that was and questioned himself.

He looked back up at her and reached for her class picture. It was all he had left of her. Pictures, mementos. He hated that, he thought as he shook his head. He hated that all he had were pictures to look at. It was as close to her as he was ever going to get.

He hated also that he had waited all these years to come back and look at them.

"She was my whole life Cain." He choked on the words as they left his lips.

Darryl, sighed a deep sigh as he covered up his trembling lips. Looking at her so clearly in the picture was different then the way his mind remembered her. He could see the blue of her eyes, the golden strands in her hair. The rosy pink of her lips.

He closed his eyes as a thought entered his mind. He could feel his thumb running across her lips. He remembered the softness of them; how he loved the way it tickled his thumb. Her lips were as soft as silk.

Darryl took another deep breath and looked back down at Cain who was looking up at him. "What are you looking at? I see the way you look at Jimmy's dog Judy. You know exactly what I'm thinking about." He chuckled at Cain and rubbed his head. In a few more days they would be back with the team and back to what would feel like normal again.

Jimmy was one of his tech specialists on his team and Judy was his dog. She loved Cain, just as much as Cain loved her.

Cain looked up at Darryl at his mention of Judy and huffed at Darryl. Darryl cocked him a grin and laughed.

He looked over toward his bed and knew under there was an old machine gun box that held more of her memories and it excited him in places he never thought it would. Movie tickets, playing cards, stacks of plays she made him read to her, napkins from the Luna Caf in town with love notes on them.

Darryl laughed at that leaning against his desk. "There are enough folded up notes in that box to put Shakespeare to shame." He told Cain as he looked over at his bed and nodded to him. "Many of which I had to steal back from my teacher's desks after getting caught with them just so I could stick them in that box, along with a lot of other things I stole from Talia."

"Come here." He said more to her memory than Cain who followed him to the bed excitedly.

He got down on his knees and pulled out the box he had left under his bed when he had left so many years ago. He sat on his floor with Cain who was watching out for him and showed him all the memories he had stored in there, tearing through the box like it was a treasure chest.

"She was really something." He told Cain sometime later, who was now passed out with his head on Darryl's knee.

Cain perked up when his commander spoke again and listened.

"She would have loved you Cain." Darryl sighed aloud looking at Cain over a stack of pictures. "You know if wasn't for her, I never would have chosen you that day we met." Darryl said looking at Cain, as he remembered the day he had met Cain.

"She used to work on weekends cleaning up the pet grooming shop in town. She loved telling me about all the different dogs and which breed she would get when we had a place of our own." Darryl remembered the little picture of the dog she had tucked into the dashboard of his SUV. He had lost that too in the accident. "She wanted a schnauzer and had a picture of a miniature schnauzer, unlike you." He thought as he looked at Cain's size and grinned. "She was grey and white, with long silky haired ears that defined her as a girl, unlike your ugly cropped and pointed ears that make you look more like a gargoyle." He laughed out loud at Cain.

"Her name she had picked out was ridiculous though. Butterfly." Darryl thought as he shook his head. "No one names their dog Butterfly." He told Cain, not even looking at him. "But Talia had a dream about the dog we would own someday together and because the dog in her dreams name was Butterfly, so her name be would be too."

Darryl remembered the way she told him excitedly about her dream like she was sitting right there in the room with them.

In my dream her ears flopped in the wind when she ran up to me just like butterfly wings, and I whispered her name Darryl and she looked right at me. Talia had said to him, sitting cross legged looking at him in his SUV when she told him. She was holding onto the picture of a dog, and it didn't matter to him what she called the dog, only that Talia would be happy and smile at him like that when he surprised her with the first miniature schnauzer puppy he could find even if he had to search the whole world over to find a little girl that looked like the dog in the picture.

Cain looked toward the door and huffed at a noise pulling Darryl thoroughly out of his own head. He barked and stood up then. Darryl commanded him to stay, and down. Cain listened and they waited for the person Darryl knew was walking toward his room.

Asher stood next to the door and leaned against the frame of it tucking his hands in his pockets.

Looking at Cain he said to Darryl, "Nothing gets to you does it?"

Darryl shook his head no, smiling, not even looking at Asher as he looked at the program from a baseball game in Toledo he had went to with Talia and Curtis and Asher, he had just pulled out of his box when Asher walked up.

Asher walked over to them and sat down. Cain ceaselessly licked his face until Darryl told him to stop.

"Who won that game?" Asher questioned him, remembering the game.

Darryl shrugged his shoulders. He couldn't remember. He had missed the end of the game because Talia had wanted to see the gift shop and buy a t-shirt before they closed for the night. They never made it to the shop and she never got her shirt. He had snuck away with her for a reason. Reasons the man in him now wanted with a desire that haunted him all the time.

He closed the book and stopped looking at it all. It had hurt to come here, he hadn't wanted too, but he honestly couldn't leave home and not come in here. He was glad he had, and he was more ashamed that Asher knew he was here then of the tears he knew where still in his eyes.

"I had a feeling when you weren't there with everyone else after the fire call I was on that you were here." Asher smiled reassuringly at him. "Your mom begged me to find you, sorry. Otherwise I would have left you alone." He said as he stretched out his legs and looked around the room. "You always did want to join the army. I just never thought it would take you away for so long." Asher sighed as he looked at the giant man Darryl had become. He wanted to get Darryl's mind out of the box he knew held memories of their past. Memories of Talia.

It was in the Stone men, to be blessed with the size they were like a curse. Their height and body left most men speechless. To look at Darryl the way he was sitting in his room, he wasn't the boy anymore that Asher remembered. He was a man now. A soldier.

Darryl set everything back in the box and pushed it under his bed where he had left it.

"Is everyone there?" Darryl questioned, rubbing his eyes and then smoothing his hair.

The Stone family was a large family, Darryl thought. He had seven aunts and uncles, more great aunts and uncles than he could count, and there were new cousins he had never met. He dreaded it, but it was his going away party. He should have been there already, he told himself.

"Yep. Everyone but you." Asher told him. His big hands he held draped over his knees, he tried to sit their resting so Darryl knew they didn't have to leave just yet if he didn't want too.

"I know why they are doing it." Darryl said to him as he rested his head on the bed behind him staring up at his old bedroom ceiling. When his eyes caught sight of a star on the ceiling he had to close his eyes. It was a glow in the dark star, one that was a part of a constellation Talia had glued to his ceiling for him to look at before he fell asleep at night.

Talia loved the stars. Her entire room had glow in the dark stars he had put up for her so she felt like she was outside while she was asleep. They had spent a lot of time working on it to get all of her favorite constellations just right. She had snuck one of them in his room so he would have a piece of her heaven to look at.

There wasn't a spot in this room that didn't remind him of her. Even the floor he was sitting on where- Darryl opened his eyes then and looked at Asher trying to remember what they had been talking about. He couldn't think of that with Asher here.

"It's more for them and their grieving then it is for me Asher. It's been that way for days. Dinners where everyone talks about Curtis." Darryl told him looking down at his hands. He had told Asher yesterday he couldn't take them anymore. "Everyone who had told me to get over Talia and move on years ago can't even do it themselves. And as much as I hate those vain feelings inside of me man, I can't look at some of them let alone be in the same room with them."

Asher started petting Cain. He hated that the two of them would be leaving and he would have to start moving on alone without them. "It's up to you man. We can stay right here if you want too."

"Can I ask you a question Asher?"

"Uncle." Asher reminded him jokingly.

Darryl smiled and wanted to laugh, but the seriousness of his question bothered him. He needed to know about Asher's girlfriend before he left. "That girl you were with…"

Asher went stone cold still. He even stopped petting Cain.

Cain looked at Asher and then at Darryl. They both felt the same way.

Asher was going to hide who ever she was and not tell him. It was written on his face he didn't want to talk about her, Darryl thought as he looked over at Asher for his answer.

"She's gone now." Asher tried to laugh it off like any other guy would do prideful. "Not sure what I did, but I pissed her off pretty good. She won't answer my calls or texts either."

Asher stilled then again. Thoughts of the woman he loved clearly running through his mind. Reasons he couldn't tell Darryl of who she was stilled him into silence.

Darryl could see he was lying about something. He was trained in interrogations. The slight rise in the blood in Asher's cheeks meant his heart was racing and his blood pressure was up. Fear of something great was causing him to not answer Darryl or talk more about her.

"Who was she?" Darryl asked offhandedly, trying to keep an ease in his voice.

Asher looked him in the eye, and for the first time in his life, he lied to Darryl. "No one."

Darryl nodded and stood up then at what he knew was a lie. If Asher was going to hide it from him, so be it. He had his answer, and there wasn't a damn thing he could do about it here.

He had a party to get too. And then he was going to get the bloody hell out of here.

Darryl was standing in the crowded living room of his grandmother's home, grasping his third bottle of cold beer. He was doing his best trying not to get drunk, but he needed more, and that was never a good thing.

He was standing next to a well-dressed cousin who just moments ago he had been introduced too, but Darryl had already forgotten his name. The young man was exhausting himself trying to explain his love for the military like Darryl had some kind of pull that would see him into the future he so desired.

"My mother told me when you were my age you wanted to join the military too. I've seen your bedroom man, it looks just like mine."

Darryl took another long sip of his beer and almost walked away from the kid. He tried not to get angry over the fact that anyone had been in that room besides him and made mental plans to have his mother put everything in his room in the attic.

Better yet, he looked for his father who he was going to tell to have it all shipped to him in Ireland.

His young cousin had yet to ask Darryl a question and he was starting to get frustrated.

Darryl listened as he talked of honor as he took another long drink of his beer. Darryl knew this kid hadn't a clue what honor meant. When he talked of the glories of war and being a soldier like he was quoting a brochure he had read from the recruitment center down the road, Darryl finally cut him a direct look, but the kid interrupted him.

"What was the hardest part of basic training for you?"

Darryl drew his eyebrows together finally frustrated. He hadn't expected this question. The more he thought of it he wanted to say leaving his family, but thoughts of what he had been through in recent years filled his mind. Darryl spoke up with urgency to his young cousin in hopes to save his life from the cruelty of this war his young mind couldn't even imagine. "Basic training is just the beginning kid. What comes after that is what makes most men throw up their lunches.

"You'll be faced with self-preservation in ways that most men cringe at. Until you are ready to be beaten and bloodied within an inch of your life as 'training', striped and left naked to die in frigid cold temperatures where your skin turns blue, to see if you can find your way out of a violent situation and see how far you can run like that. You'll be thrown out of a perfectly good plane and ship, for no reason other than to see if you can land on your feet. If you can't, then you are sadly not ready for training. Until you can walk through hell fires and come out standing on the other side hungry and braver than when you went into them, then you are not ready for war."

Darryl watched as he cringed at all the possibilities of what 'training' and 'war' was really all about. He wanted to tell him more of the horrors of training in an attempt to scare him. He had been trained to work with kids like his cousin, new recruits who had no idea what they were doing, and this is what he had told them. But Darryl knew in their present company he shouldn't.

Darryl could think of years he spent in training. Training that had made him the man he was today, but it had also stripped him of any bravery or honor he had thought he had in him when he had first joined. There wasn't a man in the military that had gone through the same thing that didn't leave them with nightmares about training.

"Basic training isn't all it's cracked up to be kid. There's no honor or glory in it. It's the time when we sort out the brats from the weak and send them packing back home to their momma's. If you survive, it's not because you are stronger than the others or better than anyone else. It is because we think you finally get it." This Darryl said looking more directly at him. "That you finally understand what it means to be a soldier. When you finally learn how to work as a team, to die as a team; then you are ready. Because one wrong move can not only get yourself killed, but everyone else standing beside you."

"When you are ready for all these things, then by all means, join. But don't sit here and talk to me and pretend you have any idea what in the hell you are getting yourself into. Because you don't. Honor and glory are for war hardened heroes and veterans. All there is for you to look forward to is hell."

Darryl's mother walked up to him then and Darryl turned to her without a last glance at his cousin.

The look in her eyes was one Darryl wished he could remove from her eyes. One he hoped his young cousin could see and understand. She had that same look the day he had left here for the Army. That look that held a thousand questions as to why he had to leave, but a smile that assured him she lovingly wouldn't ask them. She understood why. She just missed her son.

"Hey, mom." He whispered as he bent down to kiss her cheek.

Aquila looked up at her son, then back down at his partner by his side. "What time do the two of you leave in the morning?"

Darryl smiled politely at her. He had told her this, a handful of times already. "My flight leaves at 600 hours mom. Asher is going to take us so you and dad won't have too."

"We don't mind doing it, honey-" Aquila started to say to him, but Darryl interrupted her.

"Mom, I know." He interrupted her with one of his sweetest smiles for her. "But honest, Asher is just dropping me off at the front doors. You and dad wouldn't even be able to go in, let alone follow me to my plane. Security is different at the airports now." Plus, he knew his mother would be crying. Darryl couldn't handle it that early in the morning. He wanted to get out of this state as fast as he could. She wouldn't understand that. He would just have to stay here as late as his mother wanted him too tonight, and say goodbye here.

"I know." She said patting his chest and smiling up at him, trying to be strong for him as she took a hard breath. "Just promise you will come home and visit more? It was so nice seeing you home again."

Darryl sighed and nodded his head at her. He stuffed his free hand in his pocket. He didn't want to lie to her, but also didn't want to grieve her more. No mother deserved what he had done to her.

"I promise mom, first chance I get." He said like he always did.

He watched as her smile brightened with hopes of seeing him again soon, then she walked away from him to spend time with others. Darryl turned then and was glad his cousin had retreated away from him also. He looked down at his beer in his hand and hoped for the best for his cousin. No one deserved the punishment that would come along with joining the military now.

He looked out the French doors that led outside to the lighted patio and noticed Asher was outside smoking in the dark. Darryl looked down at Cain and questioned him a command. "Smoke?"

Cain all but bolted to the doors. He knew when Darryl asked this, it was time to go outside.

Darryl went out the open doors and followed Cain's lead and lit up once he was outside.

"Hey." Asher greeted him with a sideways smile once Darryl was by his side.

"I'm not interrupting am I?" Darryl asked as he watched Cain sniff around the backyard in the dark.

"No. Not at all." Asher told him, as he blew out his smoke. "I see you met Luke."

Darryl smiled at that. "Yeah." Luke, he reminded himself. That was his name. "He will make a fine Marine one day." Darryl chuckled to himself. Kids always choose the Marines when they realize they can't handle the combat of the Army.

"I heard everything you told him." Asher smiled cockily as he blew out his smoke sideways. "That's all he talks about. I've tried getting him to join the fire department more times than I can count, but all he wants is the guns and the glory."

"Like you did me?" Darryl questioned him, watching the slow burn of his smoke in his hand in the darkness of the night.

Asher smiled at that, trying not to choke on his smoke. "You had me fooled when you started coming to drills and fires. I thought I had finally broken through back then."

Darryl remembered those days. Days when he was torn between wanting to give Talia a better life than the military. He had started coming to drills and taking the radio while the guys went on calls. But he never wanted to be a firefighter. He was just grasping for straws back then.

"What made you finally decide on the Army?" Asher asked.

Darryl knew the answer to this question. He had always wanted the army. It was in his blood like firefighting was in Asher's. And then Talia had died, and his decision was made for him.

"Honestly, after she died, I just wanted to run. I couldn't live life without her. I ran to the first thing that felt right."

"Do you ever regret it?"

Darryl thought about that question too. Did he? Some days he regretted not seeing his mom, not being here for his family. Knowing the protection he provided them all now made him not regret his decision though. But he could never explain that to Asher. He took a long hit of his smoke and let it sit deep in his lungs before he spoke.

"Being here this week has shown me that I could never have made it here." He said as he stretched out his fears of what he was going to say.

"I couldn't have moved on with life. Everyone else here did, and that's good for them. But I couldn't have." He said as he flicked his smoke free from the ashes and took another hit.

"Joining was the best thing for me. It distracted me, kept me busy. Kept my mind off her," Darryl said resting his hands on the rails of the porch in front of him looking down. "I would go months not even thinking about her Asher." He looked down at what was left of his smoke and had to laugh at the memories. "Then someone would have a picture hanging on their locker and it would remind me of her and the pictures that weren't on my locker. Or someone would get a love letter from back home, and it would remind me of the all damn letters she would have been writing me had she not died." He said throwing out his smoke in the yard below him.

Darryl reached in his jean pockets then and pulled out his smokes. He lit up again and tried to forget about all the letters he had tried to write to her after he had joined. He had needed someone to talk to, but he was writing to a ghost. She would never answer him. It just became a diary of their memories.

Asher rested his arms out in front of them on the rails. "I never knew man. I never how hard it all was for you all this time." He had never heard Darryl talk about Talia like he was now either. He looked sideways at Darryl. "I'm glad you came home though man. I missed you." He grinned at Darryl and watched as he smiled also.

Darryl knew inside his self that it finally felt like home again and it made him smile. "I'm glad I did too."

They bumped fist together like they always did and returned to looking out over the darkness in the yard.

Cain sat down with a humph next to Darryl then. There was nothing interesting outside to keep his attention. Darryl smiled down at him. They would be back to work tomorrow and Cain would have plenty to do.

"You two make a fine team, Darryl. I'm glad to know someone's got your back out there." Asher told him looking proudly over to Cain who was by Darryl's side.

Darryl looked down at Cain then. Cain had been by his side for many years. Asher didn't know the half of it.

He finished his smoke outside then turned to look back through the open doors back inside his family's' home. He took a deep breath and thought of one last favor he needed from Asher before he left here. "Promise me something Asher." He asked.

"Anything. Just ask Darryl."

"No matter what happens, you'll protect them. All of them." This he said, and then turned to look at Asher for an answer.

Asher blew out his smoke and flicked away the butt into the darkness of the yard.
"It's what I do best man. You have my word. You just stay safe out there, ok?"

Darryl nodded to him as they grabbed each other's arms in a manly shake. Then walked back inside together side by side.

If Asher only knew what he was asking of Darryl, he wouldn't be letting Darryl leave in the morning. Darryl decided to leave the conversation at what it was. One man asking another man to watch over his family in his absence, but thoughts of what he had learned while he had been here haunted him, and made him wish he was leaving tonight.

He spent more time with his family then he wanted to. He took one last look, one last hug, and gave one last smile for them to remember him by.

Darryl talked to his father about where he was headed. His father, a military man himself, was the only one who understood Darryl's need for secrecy and didn't ask questions.

His grandfather, Frank hugged Darryl awkwardly in a goodbye when he left their home followed by his aunts and uncles and friends he hadn't seen in years. Darryl took on a last look at his childhood home before he got into Asher's truck and really looked at his grandparents home. It was just the way he remembered it. He hoped it would stay that way for years to come.

When Darryl boarded the plane at the metro airport in Detroit the next morning with Cain, he watched as the city lights of his home disappeared in the clouds below him, and followed the rising sun into the east as it rose above the clouds to the military base where he would find the rest of his team along with the mission he would have to complete before he could make good on his promise to his mother.

He prayed though, that he would never have to return here to Luna Pier.

Darryl sat there, headphones connected to his ears, his partner seated on the floor in front of him, staring out the window watching the world go by him at speeds he was accustomed too. He let the memories he had been running from for years run through his mind. He gave into them for what little bit of time he had left alone. He closed his eyes and tried to will Talia back into existence.

Chapter Three: Curtis' Awakening

Curtis Stone woke up in the dark. His face was against a stone floor that felt cool and chilled his body to a temperature he hadn't felt in days. Curtis listened into his mind trying to remember why that was, and where he was.

He took a long breath but the air he sucked into his lungs burned with a pain that reminded him of fire. Thoughts of a fire filled his mind. He remembered falling and hitting the ground.

Curtis kept his eyes closed tighter remembering how his bones broke when he hit the ground. He remembered the fire that consumed and burned him and wouldn't stop no matter how he screamed for it to stop.

Curtis opened his eyes then, his body couldn't feel the pain of burning flesh anymore. Not caring where he was any longer, he was only thankful the memories were just a bad dream of some sort. He tried to lift himself off the ground in the darkness, but his body felt heavy. He smelled the ground and his senses came alive. There was a dry emptiness in the breath he took again. It burned, again. Curtis really opened his eyes then, intent on finding out where he was. Where the hell was he, he wondered. But the room was dark as night.

"Well, good morning Darlin."

Curtis heard the angelic voice a woman. It startled him into stunned silence. He didn't recognize the voice, and couldn't picture the woman it belonged to in his mind. Confused he followed the voice with his eyes.

In the pitch-black of the darkness, he could see her with perfect, unknown clarity. Who she was he didn't know, but his body responded to the woman in the red dress sitting prettily in front of him. When his body responded, his skin came alive. It was burning still. Every inch of his entire body felt like it was on fire then.

Curtis curled up there on the floor and hugged his body tight. The burning was engulfing him. Again.

The woman in the room with him started talking to someone else in the room, a man, Curtis could sense. But he didn't care who they were, all he could feel was the pain in his body.

"He's going to need more time, Joseph." Curtis heard the woman say.

"I can see that." This time, the man's voice, Curtis could hear more clearly. He didn't recognize either one of them.

Curtis looked up at the woman longer this time. He didn't understand why she was just sitting there at a table watching him in agonizing pain. Was she sipping on a glass?

Curtis didn't know who she was but a desire was boiling up inside of him to strangle her. Who was she? Why had she brought him here? Why was he hurting so damn badly?

"You are going to feel like that for a couple more days." She said to him more quietly, sounding like she was trying to reassure him of something.

Curtis didn't understand who she was, and he didn't trust her at all. His instincts had never steered him wrong before, and right now they were telling him to run.

Curtis fell all the way back down to the cold ground and let his face touch the floor so he could feel the cold there on his cheek.

He looked over at her again and watched as she shook her head at him in way that condemned him. He watched as she took another long sip of her glass. She licked her lips and savored the tasted there. She picked up the glass and unwound her legs from each other and stood up. She walked seductively over to Curtis who was now trying to crawl away from her in fear.

She tipped the glass down toward him while she sensually bent down in front of him. She blew the scent of it towards him. "Smell that?" She questioned him.

Curtis had to stop backing away from her, he had reached a stone-cold wall, and there was nowhere else to go. As afraid of her as he was, the smell of the contents in her drink consumed him, filled his nostrils and stopped all his thoughts of escape. Curtis turned his head back toward her in acknowledgment. He knew that smell all too well. Years of fire service had taught him what it was. Blood.

But why… Why did the smell of blood ignite a hunger within him he couldn't control?

"Ah. There you go." She said to him with a smile of admiration that confused Curtis. She stood up then and walked back over to the table and filled the glass full of more blood. She turned back to Curtis and cocked her head at him. She took a seductive sip and pointed it back at him. "Want some?"

Curtis had to lick his dry lips. It didn't help; his tongue was dry too. He knew, he really knew that he didn't want what was in that glass. But...

"This," She told him as she walked sensually back over to him. "This is your life source now." She bent down then again in front of him. "What you feel in your body now-"

"All I feel is pain!" Curtis interrupted her, hollering as loudly as he could, angered, but his voice was so hoarse that it hurt and he struggled to finish his sentence.

"Like I was saying, what you feel inside of you is your life being sucked out of you. Your body will heal. You need this," she told him sloshing the drink around in the glass in front of him. "To help you heal."

She had appeared in front of him in a blink of an eye. Her whispered words confused him more. Curtis closed his eyes and lay back down exhausted, so he put his face back on the cold floor. "No." he whispered.

She stood up then. Curtis raised an eye at her curiously watching her leave.

"Suit yourself." She said to him as she walked back over to the table and resumed her seat, folding one leg sexually over the other. She held the glass up to her lips and smiled over to him. "More for me. I got all the time in the world Darlin."

Shelley waited for what like felt hours. Days even. Wondering when Curtis would relent. She could just picture him coming over to the table and drinking heavily of the blood she had waiting for him. She knew in that moment, he would be hers.

She waited then, and then waited longer. He was powerful enough now to get up on his own. She had no idea why he wasn't doing it. She honestly thought the temptation of her drinking herself full would do it for him. But, in the end, it hadn't. Not even the smell of the blood that she knew was tempting was enough to break him.

Curtis Stone was indeed a very strong man.

Emie Whitby walked into the dungeon a few days later. One of Shelley's closest and dearest friends. Shelley was still sitting there keeping watch over Curtis.

"You need to get him out of here, Shelley." Emie begged her as she stood next to the table shaking her head at him in disbelief.

Shelley knew Emie didn't agree with her and Joseph on this, but Shelley knew from her visions that one day soon Emie would.

Shelley looked at her friend in question. "Go play with your human! This one is mine." Shelley told Emie.

Emie looked at her in disgust then. She couldn't believe Shelley and Joseph had done this to her. Not only had Joseph scared the hell out of Curtis' brother Asher before the funeral and ruined all their chances together, but now he had taken the life of Curtis.

"You will understand this all of this soon sweetie. I promise." Shelley told her, not even looking at her. And this Shelley knew because she had seen it. It would feel like forever to Emie, and Shelley hated that she had to do this to her, but what was about to happen was going to happen one way or another.

Emie turned and walked back to the stairs. She couldn't stay in this house any longer and Shelley didn't fault her for it.

Curtis was listening to their exchange. Shelley could see it all in his mind. He didn't understand it all. He wondered why they had him here instead of being in the hospital.

She started to tap on her glass with one of her long, red fingernails and eyed him curiously. When they locked eyes, he realized who she was. He remembered her from the hospital. In his waking hours of agony there, he remembered her.

This made Shelley smile.

Curtis waited for death, but it never came.

Chapter Four: Mission

500th Military Intelligence Brigade
US Army Post, North Carolina
Fort Bragg

Darryl was leaning up against a table in the hangar of an army military air base in Fayetteville North Carolina, and watched as the sunset disappeared out of the open doors. He was waiting for the moment his team would walk through the wide-open doors in front of him. It would be business as usual once everyone settled down and got back to work.

The vampiric enemy Darryl and his team had been hunting down for so many years in the east had finally made its way across the globe to their homeland. There was no stopping it now.

This new mission was one Darryl was unsure they would walk away from. The more swarms of vampires they found, the worse it got. The island they were going to, well, no one knew what was waiting for them there. No one had been there yet.

Why the enemy was there was the most important part of his mission. He had learned from army intel that there were scientists on that island that the enemies were looking to kidnap. Darryl and his team needed to rescue those scientists as quickly as possible.

Darryl gave himself one last free moment, knowing in the coming months, even years, he would never have this much freedom again. Intel had filled him in with new information he was dreading sharing with his men. He took a deep breath and let his mind wander away from his mission one last time.

Darryl lit up a smoke and inhaled deeply; he stretched his legs out on the cement floor in front of him and looked down. He wanted more time to himself then just these last few moments, he thought. He was dressed in his black Special Ops military edition t-shirt, black cargo pants and black combat boots. He dragged his hand through his jet-black military cut hair. He looked and felt Army. It was a special kind of adrenaline high knowing what he was about to do, but it was his childhood memories of Talia that was the high he longed to be on right now.

Darryl closed his eyes and thought of home. He sighed quietly to himself as thoughts of Talia entered his mind.

Home. He thought as he smoked his smoke. He was worried about his home and had to fight the fears he was having and had to point his attention out the doors to where his men would be soon so he could lead them, guide them and direct them, or there would be no home left for any of them to return too.

Cain was laying on his duffle bags on the floor in front of Darryl, waiting for his commands. Darryl smiled and allowed him to just lay there. Cain too needed this moment.

They hadn't donned their steel armor yet, but soon, once aboard the plane that would take them to the deserted island they would be stationed at, they would have to put it on.

Steel was the only thing that could protect them from their enemy. Steel was the thing that had kept the two of them alive these years, Darryl thought as he looked at the cargo boxes that held his and Cain's armor and weapons. He dreaded wearing the damn heavy things again.

In a few moments, Darryl thought to himself, they would be boarding a plane that would take them off their homeland soil, to a place that was dark and cold every day. If they didn't die at the hands of the enemy, they might freeze to death in the rigorous climate. Or go crazy in the endless darkness of the days ahead of them.

Darryl flicked out his smoke thinking about it. He hated the cold. It reminded him of winters at home in Michigan. He would take the winters anywhere else in this world close to the equators, but in any direction north or south of them, Darryl hated. Why he had to spend so much time in the north all these years he would never understand, and now that he was going to the very southernmost part of the Earth, he regretted going back to DC for his orders.

The enemy lived in the coldest, darkest places on this earth, where they could hide from the sun, and be invisible to the world around them. Darryl had lived these many years in those cold, dark places, extricating the enemy from where they had sought solace, hunting them down and destroying them from the face of this earth.

Darryl lit one last smoke. He inhaled deeply and let the nicotine take away his fears. He knew he was a killer. A hunter of monsters. Those thoughts troubled him deeply sometimes. He tried to remind himself why he was who he was. He was a soldier, and a protector he reminded himself. He was defender of his people, his land, and his home. He was also, now, a soldier fighting a war to save the rest of the world, he reminded himself.

He had traveled all over this world back and forth while in the Army. It was nothing for him to travel now, he was used to it. By jet, ship, plane or anything else he was put on that moved him around this world in the army, it was almost second nature to him. His only regret was not spending more time taking in the scenery in most places he had been.

And not spending more time at home with his family.

Home… Darryl tried to shake it off as he looked at his watch. Any moment now his men would be walking toward him, he even looked up to make sure they weren't yet.

He wasn't ready to stop thinking about home though. He wasn't ready to let go of it just yet. He had always thought of home as a place where Talia had died. Now it was home again. Talia's memory no longer lived there. She was in his heart again.

His mother had packed up his things like he asked her too and she had mailed him the box the day after he had left. He would take Talia's memories everywhere with him now like the picture he kept in his pocket. But it was his family; his mother, his uncle, his grandmother, Talia's brother Ken. They were his home now. He missed them already.

Thoughts of his mission plagued his mind then again as he watched his men walking toward him through the hangar doors in front of him. His stomach started to do flips and his mouth went dry. He might never see home again, but his feet were now firmly planted on the ground he was sworn to protect. He would give his all and protect the ones he loved. He had a new mission now in his heart. A mission to save the ones that mattered most in his life, and to not die trying. He had to protect his home. They needed to be saved.

Bartley was the first of his team to shake and bump fist with Darryl as he threw his bag on the ground next to Darryl's. Bartley stood a head taller than Darryl. His black army t-shirt sleeves were rolled up tight on his tattooed arms. His red, Irish hair was spiked thick on top of his military crew cut.

His dog, Sentry, a military pitwiller, trained in search and rescue, met Cain with eagerness. Darryl and Bartley watched as the two circled each other and hopped around like old friends. They took off together for Judy who was now walking next to Jimmy through the open doors.

Darryl looked over his men as Judy, Jimmy's dog, a Belgian Malinois, joined Cain and Sentry in greeting. Jimmy threw his bags next to the team's bags, sat on the ground and pulled his tablet off his arm ready to take notes. He was dressed and eager, Darryl could tell, ready to get to work.

Jimmy was small in stature compared to the rest of the men. He was built like a machine though; hard and ready for war, but his tech glasses and attachments made him look like he was more suited for desk work.

Darryl noticed the bluetooth in Jimmy's ear. The blue light that shined after Jimmy turned it on was a remote link to the base. Gavin, their remote computer specialist at the base was waiting and ready on the line for his commands also. Gavin and Jimmy stayed in constant contact with the team and with each other via the tablets they all carried on their arms and the bluetooth's they all wore in their ears. Darryl only wore his when they were in battle or out on a raid, so Gavin always requested to be on speaker so he could be heard by Darryl when he wasn't wearing his.

Darryl hated Gavin with a passion. He shook his head and realized the gravity of that hatred as he crossed his arms and wiped his mouth with an unsteady hand. Gavin's endless, distasteful banter about sex and women, along with his mightier than thou attitude drove Darryl to day dreaming about beating Gavin with all his tech savvy equipment. Gavin was the one and only thing Darryl hadn't missed while he was at home.

Patrick was now standing next to Jimmy, Darryl noticed, his legs spread apart in perfect military position with his arms held behind his back, looking full and ready for a fight dressed in his black, steel armor and combat boots. Darryl, Jimmy and Bartley had chosen to hold off on putting on their steel armor that helped them fight the enemies, but Darryl had to smile at Patrick for his readiness and wondered if he had worn it the entire time he had been off duty. The thought of it made Darryl shake his head and laugh out loud as he met young Patrick's fist with a bump, trying to break him of his proud posture.

Johnny and Toby stood next to Patrick. They were twins, hard for even Darryl to tell apart; they were ready also. The three of them came to Darryl's team from Ireland late last year after Darryl had lost members of his first team learning how to fight this war. They had all spent time together while in Ireland training and preparing better for this war ahead of them. Now they were fully equipped, fully hard, and ready for war.

Pat knew firsthand how to fight the enemy and had brought to the team the steel armor they all wore, including the armor for the dogs, Sentry, Judy and Cain. The heavy steel metal was heavy, but it was impenetrable by the vampires.

Johnny and Toby were Darryl's gun specialists. Each designed and carried steel weapons throughout their gear. They kept Darryl's team equipped with the right tools to fight with and were always ready to spray fire and steel on the blood sucking vampires they encountered.

Skelly, also known as Mike was walking slower than the rest up to Darryl, talking on his phone like he hadn't a care in the world, smoking and drinking out of a flask. He was still dressed in civilian clothes Darryl noticed. His blonde hair was scattered and all out of place and his hair length was never up to military standards and it always bothered Darryl. Darryl knew he should say something about Skelly's attire, but he also knew the command would be lost on Skelly.

There was no telling Skelly what to do, no punishment great enough. He worked at his own pace, even if it was against the rules. Skelly was as close to a section 8 as they came, longing to be anywhere else then the career path he had foolishly chosen, and he cared less one way or the other on how he could escape his duties.

Darryl noticed Skelly reeked of smoke and beer and something else foul when he shook Darryl's hand, ignoring Darryl completely as he finished up his conversation and tucked away his phone.

Darryl shook his head ashamed as he watched Skelly.

Each man knew why they were here Darryl thought as he looked them all over with a sigh, glad to see each one of them again. They never spent much time apart, and when they did, it was nice to be back together again as a team. There were no other men that Darryl wanted beside him fighting, he thought quietly.

Darryl had left them in Ireland to spend time with his family in Michigan. They were here now in the states, back from their own homes, ready for their next mission.

The enemy was waiting for them. And they were ready for battle. Blood thirsty and war bound.

"I hope everyone is rested and enjoyed some much needed vacation time." Darryl said to them in a commanding tone, greeting them.

"How's your family man?" Bartley, Darryl's second in command and a good friend asked.

"Good, thank you." Darryl said smiling knowingly in a silent thank you to Bartley. Darryl had never had a friend like Bartley. Bartley was trained in how to be a commander's second and knew his role well, but it was the extra mile he always seemed to go for Darryl that had sealed their trust and made their friendship easy.

Jimmy's speakers came to life and the voice of Gavin spoke loudly over the speakers. "Technically, it wasn't a vacation. But needed nonetheless."

No one commented on Gavin's reply to Darryl. It was the way he viciously bantered with Darryl that made all the men silent at times. It was that, that made Darryl want to do bodily harm to the man.

Vacation time was never meant to be spent with family. This they all knew well. That is just what Darryl had called it and commanded them all to do before he had left them. Spend time with family; it might be the last chance to do so.

Technician and half-witted genius that Gavin was, he always knew when to chime in. Something Darryl loathed as his commander. It was Gavin's job to seek out their mission and relay back the information they would need, such as locations and top secret information no one else had. Darryl needed Gavin, in ways he hated to admit.

Darryl looked at what was left of his last smoke and flicked it away from him. It was time to get down to business.

"Intel is sending us to the Amundsen-Scott South pole station."

Darryl raised his hand when everyone looked up at him and started talking at once, cussing him out.

"There are reports that some of the workers have gone missing out of the station. Intel wants us to scope things out. One of the security team members stationed by the army, seen one of the vamps and reported it before he also went missing.

"There is a team of top scientists down there that have been studying the demographics of the ice life on the island. They are the reason the enemy is there. We need to clear the scientists out and send them to Washington where they are needed and then get the hell out of there."

Gavin chose that moment to chime in, interrupting Darryl. "There are 150 workers in that station. The continent is 2,835 meters above sea level. There are no roads in or out of that station. How does Intel expect us to evacuate a station of that size? By ship?   By plane? We will never make it through the storms down there this time of year, let alone make it across the island without losing the whole crew in the darkness of days."

"And, not to mention, it's minus eighty-one fucking degrees down there today!"

Darryl sighed greatly and stopped breathing as he rubbed his eyes with one hand. He could hear that Gavin had thrown something in frustration over the speakers. He watched now as each man looked at him for answers he couldn't give them. He knew sometimes their missions were dangerous, and that they were not to save the lives of the many, but only of the few. The most important few. Explaining that to men who were trained to save everyone was hard. Not being able to strangle Gavin with his wires was harder.

"17 of the 150 have gone missing. 10 of those missing are women." Darryl let that sink in for Gavin. He noted that Gavin didn't chime back in.

"Bloody Hell." Bartley said to Darryl's expression. "What do they expect us to do?"

Darryl knew from what they had learned in the past that there was nothing they could do now for those who were missing. They were either killed for their blood, or they had been turned into the enemy by now. Worse things would happen to the women, and for that reason Darryl knew his men would fight harder now.

"There is a group of engineers going with us. They are going to install new lamp posts around the station. These new posts they will be installing are secretly designed with cameras as a remote link to an Army ship off shore that will be monitored by Intel.

"No one, from the engineers who will be joining us, from the crew at the station, down to the lead scientist that is there; no one is to know anything about who we are, what we do, or why we are there."

Darryl trusted his team, and knew those words didn't need to be said, but he said them anyways. What they all were, who they all were, was a secret to the world. They were hunters, killers, protectors in secret to an unknown enemy of the world. It wasn't their first mission, and it wouldn't be their last. Darryl now had a new separate folder on his tablet filled with new information that was going to take him and his team at least a year to complete.

"Bartley and I have to cover the engineers so they can get the work done outside. Toby and Johnny will assist in setting up cameras throughout the inside of the station. Jimmy and Pat will be installing new computers in the buildings and video surveillance.

"The station is expecting us. They believe we are assisting the coast guard and the scientists who are down there studying, so our guns and armor won't seem out of place. They believe they are being attacked by polar bears or wolves. There has even been a report of a snow monster." He said aloud to his men, knowingly at their chuckles.

Gavin chimed back in. "Nothing lives there. No bears, no wolves. There aren't even bugs there. Those scientists should know that.

"Why the fuck are we installing cameras?"

Darryl scratched his head. He had never met Gavin in person, and for the first time ever, Darryl wished he was accompanying them on this mission so he could wrap his hand around Gavin's neck, just once, when he made an outburst like that. Gavin was never on the missions with them in person except remotely through the cameras Jimmy wore around his neck. There were many times that Darryl wanted to rip the attachments to Jimmy's arm off and throw it as far as he could.

Darryl sighed greatly and looked at his men. Each man looked away from Darryl then. They knew what their mission entailed. Escape the few, protect the rest. The ones they couldn't protect, would be left there as bait. They had survived the first wave; the second would wipe them off the face of the map.

Darryl didn't have to explain it them, he could see it on their faces as he watched them. His men hated this as much as he did.

Jimmy looked at Judy and had her sit next to him. She licked his face in response. "What about the dogs? If it's that cold there, what will they do?"

Darryl sat back against the table and looked toward Cain and Sentry who were lounging on the duffle bags. He hated Jimmy's constant worry over the dogs. They were officers in the Army. No different than any of them.

Darryl sighed again deeply. As much as that was true, he couldn't deny his own worry over Cain. He had lost men before under his command, but never a close, personal friend like Cain had become.

"We need them with us inside the station to alert us if the enemy makes it inside. When we go outside, they will have to wear special suits designed for them along with their steel armor.

"You will all depart from the island on July 29th to a remote ship in the ocean where we will study the enemy as it swarms through after we leave. Once they find out we have left, and there is still a crew there, we hope they will overtake it. If we are to defeat this enemy in our home land, we have to study them before they get here. Learn what we have failed to understand in the past." This last part he told them because of the looks on his team's' faces. He knew they wouldn't agree to this, but they would have too. They would have to watch as the vamps destroyed them all. It was an order.

"Jimmy, Johnny, Toby and Pat. Start filling the plane. Make sure we have everything." He said to them nodding at the boxes of cargo next to their plane in the hangar.

"Bartley, get the dogs in their cages and ready for transport. Jimmy, you and Gavin do some Intel on the scientist during the flight. Find out who we are dealing with there. I want to know everyone on that continent, no surprises.

"We leave at 1300 hours."

Darryl picked up his tablet and pushed send on the program that would send the mission folder to each man's tablet. Each man had a job to do and mission to follow. He watched as each man looked at their own tablets. He trusted them, but he also worried for them. This mission would be harder than any other in their past together.

Bartley scoffed his boots as the rest of the men started moving. "There's no sun?" he questioned Darryl.

Darryl put his hand on his friend's shoulder. "More time to play." He winked at Bartley.

They shared a smirk, and started packing.

July 29th 2015

Darryl was sitting next to Cain on the floor of the engineering room on the 'Polar Ship' manned by the US coast guard. He was lost in thought, smoking, worried.

They were to be stationed in the Mozambique Channel now near Madagascar, but Darryl had to wait for the rest of his team before they could depart for safer waters. His team was supposed to be now returning on a helicopter coming from the island of Antarctica.

They were late.

Darryl hadn't heard from them in three days, and he was starting to worry.

He had completed his mission of delivering the scientist to Washington DC, and had left the crew in the station like he had been ordered to do. There was a total of twenty-eight people left. Twenty-eight people whose lives and destruction would be left in his hands. They were all unaware of what was coming.

His men had been left there also while he had delivered the scientist to safety. They were all headed to him now on the ship, where they would watch the destruction of the island.

Cooks, janitors, doctors, nurses, two young botanists and a tour guide were all that was left on the continent. Darryl would forever see them in his dreams now. Sure, he had lost people before, helpless people he couldn't save. But these innocent station members, who he had come to know over the recent weeks, were about to die at the hands of a vengeful vampiric army who cared not at all about humanity. They were searching for blood. They would take their time destroying each member, like in the times past that Darryl and his team had witnessed. And Darryl wouldn't be able to stop them this time.

Worse, he was going to have to watch it.

Darryl listened as the door behind him opened and he heard the unmistakable foot fall of a man in combat boots approached him. It relieved him like air returning to his lungs. Even Cain was wagging his tail as he listened too.

Bartley sat down next to them, sinking to the floor, pulling Darryl away from his worrisome thoughts along with his smoke that Bartley took a long hit from.

Darryl hadn't seen his team in three days. Three days Darryl spent on this ship waiting for word of their return. He sighed and welcomed his friend back at his side.

"Report?" He asked Bartley, not looking at him as he took his smoke back and flicked what was left of it on the floor of the ship.

Bartley wasn't looking at Darryl either. "We lost Skelly."

Darryl looked at Bartley then. He wasn't surprised, but yet he was. Skelly had never listened to any of his commands let alone listen to Bartley's. Skelly was careless and thoughtless.

"What happened?" Darryl's asked anyways.

"We were all packing up the helicopter two days ago, when Rager, one of the docs at the station came walking out with some of the other station members. He started arguing with us that we were leaving them all to die."

Both Darryl and Bartley knew it had been bound to happen. That didn't surprise Darryl at all.

"You remember that story the doctors were telling us about some unknown snow monster they were all afraid of?"

"How could I forget? That's all they talked about." Darryl remembered, as he rubbed his head. Little did they know that there were things out there worse than snow monster's. Even the dogs had known what was out there beyond the station.

"Well, Rager started this in front of the pilots. Shouting at them that they couldn't leave and abandon them there. Next thing I know Skelly is walking off the chopper raving about how the members knew what was really going on. How the truth was finally coming out."

Darryl could see it all playing out in his mind. Skelly, inching away from the team. Leaving himself and the team vulnerable.

"One by one, Skelly, two nurses, and a doctor got picked off. Johnny got two of the vamps in the head, but Toby lost his footing and got dragged a half of a mile before Johnny could get a shot at them and get them off Toby.

"Toby's fine," he reassured Darryl, looking sideways at him. "Got a little scratched up in the face. He's just mad about Skelly though." Bartley looked away from Darryl then and down at his hands he had resting on his knees folded together. "We were all paying attention Darryl. I swear. We were watching out even though the doctors were shouting at us. It was Skelly who flipped out and distracted us all."

Darryl nodded his head as he listened to Bartley. He completely understood about Skelly. "It's ok. I know. Anything else?" He waited, and then worried when Bartley didn't speak up right away.

Bartley turned his head and looked at his commander. "I found out yesterday, from Rager, after we finally had every one calmed down, that Skelly had been talking to Rager."

"Rager used to be special ops in the marines. He knew something was up when we showed up in armor with weapons." Bartley explained to Darryl.

"I knew he was going to be dangerous to the mission by what all he was revealing to us that Skelly had told him. He's with us now. We took him because Skelly had said too much in front of him before he died. The pilots will need to be dealt with too, along with Rager."

"What about the others?" Darryl questioned him urgently.

"The rest of the members at the station will find the dead bodies soon of the other members that were killed that day and think Rager got drug off by that monster also."

"They have their suspicions, but it shouldn't affect the mission none."

Darryl was tired, he realized as Bartley finished. He knew the worst was ready to begin now that they weren't there on the island anymore. He had a lot to do with Gavin and Jimmy in the next few days and he was not looking forward to it. He would deal with the loss of one of his men later. There was nothing to be done about the rumors or lives that were lost, or their silly suspicions. That was going to have to be the Army's problem, not his.

"Get Rager ready for interrogation. Make sure the room is away from the sailors on the ship. If he's lucky and survives us, now that he knows about us, maybe we can use him on the team. Get Gavin on it," Darryl said as he thought more about it. "I want to know everything about the man. Did any of the pilots see what happened during the attack?"

"Yeah. I'll get them ready too." Bartley said as he got to his feet. He turned back to look at Darryl. He knew Darryl had been through enough back home. This mission had taken its toll on his friend. He could see it in Darryl's eyes how tired and worn he really was. "When you were home…" He started to ask Darryl, trying to pull him out of his mood.

Darryl looked up at Bartley then. He knew what his friend wanted. He interrupted him and pulled out the picture of Talia he had kept safe with him.

Bartley had joked around with Darryl their whole friendship that Darryl was either gay or lying about Talia. Darryl was the only guy in the team who never needed a woman, or talked about sex. Gavin had said out loud in front of everyone that Talia never existed and Darryl had made her up, which had only earned Bartley a busted lip one drunken night with Darryl. Bartley had apologized for ever speaking of the matter in front of Gavin later the next day to Darryl, but Darryl had promised proof of her existence the next time he went home just to clear the air.

Dumbfounded, Bartley looked at the picture in Darryl's hand. He took it from him and made no comment except that he looked at the picture longer then Darryl liked.

Darryl knew the picture by heart. He could still feel Talia in his arms the way he was holding her. He could still smell the freshness of her hair as she leaned in close to his face and closed her eyes.

Bartley handed him the picture back that Darryl had pulled off the poster at the funeral. Darryl looked at it again. He traced her face and looked at Curtis in the picture. He missed them both so much.

Bartley stood up tall and stretched. "Yeah, she's worth it." Bartley grinned shyly and walked away.

Darryl smiled knowingly. Bartley had once told him there was no woman worth the life Darryl had chosen to live. Now that he seen the woman Darryl had been with, he understood.

Darryl stood up and walked over to the captain of the ship. "Take us out of here. Now."

Darryl stood at the front windows of the ship and looked out into the darkness of the ocean night in front of them. He thought of how Jimmy and Gavin would spend the next two days showing Darryl the footage of the station. He didn't want to be here anymore. He watched as the ship left the island and he bid it farewell.

It was three days later when they had docked in Madagascar that the attacks happened. Gavin recorded everything. Darryl and his men sat and watched as it unfolded. Baffled, by everything that they had missed in the past.

Gavin was able to playback the worst, and with the new high tech cameras they had installed, he was able to zoom in and see the vamps with more clarity. How they fought. What they went after first. How they unknowingly killed and fed while being watched.

What his team hadn't been prepared for, or to watch, was the demons that were there overhead. Flying around with claw like appendages that could sever a man's head off with one swing.

Chapter Five: The Difference

Christmas, December 2015

     Shelley was sitting out by the shore on the panhandle of Florida's coast, in Navarre Beach. She had been out here in the darkness for hours, alone, mad at Curtis. She was waiting subconsciously for her friend, Jordy Whitby, Emie's younger brother, to arrive while she watched the eclipse in front of her over the water.

     Curtis Stone, her newest project, had taken to her world in the form of a time shifter. Something she had never dreamed possible. Hungry for all things vampire-ish, even though he hated his new life.

     Curtis was not the first human she had turned into a vampire, but he was sure to be the last. Shelley had enough of training young vampires. It wasn't easy. And Curtis had been one of her hardest students.

     Shelley twisted her long, red curls as she waited, completely unfazed by the beauty of the eclipse that night. Any moment now, she knew, Jordy would appear next to her out here. He was troubled. And troubled he should be. With the way the world was now, and also because of his sister, Emie Whitby, who had gone missing months ago.

Many of the world's population had gone missing recently. To the rest the world, Emie was just another statistic. But to her family, she was missed deeply.

Shelley missed her best friend Emie, yes. But she also knew the reasons she had went into hiding. A place Shelley wished she could run to as well. Emie was running away from Asher. She was trying to make the right decisions, vampire that she was, and not be in his life, even though she loved him with a passion that surpassed anything or anyone Shelley had ever known.

She sighed then and looked down at her hands in her lap. Learning and telling the future had always haunted Shelley. Deciding to be the one to change Curtis so the Whitby family didn't get caught up there in Luna Pier alone without any help, had been what she had thought was a good idea. They needed a hero, and Curtis was as good as any.

He wasn't a white knight on a fiery steed, but he could drive a fire truck like no one else. He wasn't a God, but he sure looked like one, Shelley thought to herself making her smile. He was strong and was fast, but Curtis had become something none of them had seen before. He had learned to disappear and stay gone for moments. Moments that would make Shelley worry.

Curtis was so adamant about this life being wrong; he refused to see them all for who they really were. He refused to even listen to her, Shelley thought more as she sighed again.

Sure they had been hard on him at first, and she had over done it a little with him in the beginning.

If Curtis would just stop for a moment and listen to them though, she thought as she waited for Jordy who she hoped could fix this, he would understand what was really at stake here.

Who wouldn't want to be the woman by Curtis' side? She had been trying to tell herself this since she had met him. He was tall, and strong. Was she really a fool for thinking he would sweep her off her feet? He was a hero even! As real as any came.

A hero… Shelley shook her head at her thoughts. Curtis was some kind of wonderful. Someone she enjoyed getting lost in him. She could listen into his heart and mind for hours while he sat out here in her chairs trying to remember his past. She loved the fantasies she created in her mind of him.

Shelley had never been one to gloat or boast about her own beauty. She had vainly assumed Curtis would fall for her and she would gain not only the perfect hero, but also the love of an honorable man. She had pictured herself finally settling down with someone. With Curtis.

She had never been so wrong in her existence. Curtis was further from her now then what he had been when he had first awoken to this new life and had clung to her for a lifeline.

Now, she thought as she sighed into the moonlit darkness around her, now Curtis was a shell of his former self. He had felt everything from pain, to hate, to blood lust. She had never imagined the man he had been would become the monster he was now.

His black, burnt body had healed and he was now the bodily perfection of a God, but his soul and heart… Shelley looked up to the heavens then. She closed her eyes and prayed she hadn't made the wrong decision.

Suddenly, like a falling star from the heavens, Jordy appeared in the chair next to her.

"He will be fine, Shell. I promise." Jordy said to her in his sweet manner.

Shelley looked at the man who was still a child in her mind. She grinned at his gorgeous, crooked smile she had missed.

Jordy's signature blonde, spiky hair that reminded her of his other Whitby brothers, Jeremy his twin, and Joseph the oldest, had never lost its style throughout the centuries. From the late 1800's till now.

He was tall like Curtis, but his powerful lean form was not to be misunderstood or reckoned with. Jordy was not only a shifter like Curtis, he could also reform matter and pass through it. His knowledge and visions of the future surpassed hers. Only because of the wisdom he bestowed with it. Jordy was not only a seer; he was also the most compassionate, understanding gentleman she had met in 6000 years. His mind reading abilities, like hers, were strong. He could hear and talk to his brothers and sister, and even Shelley from anywhere in the world.

There was a time when she had thought he was one of a kind, until she had met Curtis.

Shelley listened into Jordy's mind then. She knew he was right about Curtis; she just couldn't shake the feelings, and not being able to see this uncertain future with Curtis bothered her in ways she couldn't explain. Jordy had not yet spent enough time with Curtis to understand her feelings fully.

Shelley looked back up at heaven. "So what's up Jordy? What do I owe the pleasure of this visit?"

Jordy's brother Jeremy had just visited two a few days ago. They were both searching for their sister Emie.

Jordy knew she knew why he was here. She was asking him aloud because it was a pleasantry gesture they all shared that made them seem more human. They all respected it.

Jordy was sitting in the way she was, looking toward the heavens for the answers they both needed. The world was falling away to hell in a handbasket. Worse was to come. He had a plan, but he needed everyone's help.

"It's Emie and Asher."

Shelley acknowledged him. They shared the same visions of them then.

"When she comes home, she and Asher will make amends; you and Curtis will need to come home then. Asher needs to know about Curtis. He needs to learn the plans we have."

Shelley chuckled at that. It was a bargain assuming Asher would take this well. He had learned Emie was a vampire just before Curtis' funeral. Curtis was his brother; Asher had mourned his death all while Emie had stood by his side, knowing full well that Curtis was alive. Asher was not going to take this knowledge well. Whether he truly loved Emie or not, he was still only a mere mortal. He couldn't understand the way they lived even if he tried.

And neither would Curtis.

"He's not ready Jordy."

"Make him."

Shelley laughed at that. "That's easier said than done Jordy." She scoffed at him.

Jordy smiled up at the night sky. "You, the bold and mighty force, the powerful Shelley! You can't make him?" this last he said turning his head over to her eyeing her sheepishly.

Shelley stopped him with her thoughts as she turned her head toward him. She stared him down then.

"Shelley listen; there is more at stake here then just Emie's well-being and some foolish love story. Luna Pier needs our help. We have spent centuries protecting and building that city to all it has become. We know the citizens there. We have friends there Shelley." He gently explained to her. "We can't just stand by and let it be destroyed by this war."

Shelley hadn't meant to laugh in her cold glass of blood she was sipping on. She wiped off her chin and looked at him. "You really think you can do anything? That we can do anything against them?" She asked him looking point blankly at him.

Shelley leaned more forward toward him. "I've seen this before Jordy. Ancient history books have never gotten it right." She said quietly remembering what they had told. Humans either denied the truth about vampires, or only told the stories in secret to protect the innocent. "During the past wars, when we would help the humans win, they would turn against us and hunt us down, then they would bury us with our heads in our hands Jordy!"

"This new generation has never seen vampires or a war like this. They don't believe in us or the stories of the evil ones, and they are either too dumb or stupid to do anything about it."

"These vampiric forces coming know what they are doing. There is a royal family older than I at work here. They seek more than just human destruction. They seek to be rulers of this world. To trod down the humans and own them for their own pleasures. Right now, they are just feeling things out. Worse is coming. Something unlike you or I have ever witnessed."

"The only reason the whole world is able to talk about all that is going on in the world together as a society now is because of the new technology they have. The media is having a field day with it. The internet is all abuzz about it."

"What they don't know, is that this family is watching it, and using it against them. They are using their fears. They will use all their abilities to destroy the humans any way they can."

"Our job here isn't to protect just one mere city. And that is what we have failed to see. While they are building armies of destruction, we should have been building armies of protection. But instead we have fallen short of that order, we have found pleasures on this Earth we were never supposed to find. We have sought out safety not in numbers, but alone in solitude. Enjoying pleasures that were meant just for humans."

"I am no one to be judging anyone Jordy. Look around you. I've spent years here, building that glorious house behind you, flying my plane all over this entire Earth, enjoying the spoils of my labor. All of which your family is guilty of too." She reminded him.

The Whitby's had discovered more treasures in this world than any other in history. She couldn't fault them for it. They had a lifetime of savings stored up, but they also spent where most men would not. They helped mankind, and built cities that even she marveled at.

Jordy took a minute to himself then. He looked away guilty as she had made him feel so frail. He looked down at his hands then and held them over his knees.

"Is it Asher's sister that plagues you the most?" She asked him.

Jordy looked in her direction stunned. Her powers never ceased to amaze him.

"So you've seen it too." He questioned.

Shelley smiled at him over her drink as she took another sip.

"I can't possibly follow through with it." Jordy said to her quietly as he sighed and looked over the waves that were rolling on the shore in front of them. He had a vision of a young woman he would fall in love with long ago. Her face and posture always haunted him. He always dreamed of the love he would share with her. But when he had met Asher's sister, and seen that it was her, Jordy feared what it would do to Asher.

"Not follow through with it? It is all you think about, ever since I met you."

Jordy laughed at that looking at his hands. "Have you met Asher?"

"He's a mere mortal. You can take him."

"Not for long…" Jordy stated simply.

Both Shelley and Jordy turned at a rustling noise behind them. Not much escaped their notice, and when it did, the surprise was astounding.

"It's Curtis." Shelley explained looking behind them. She could here inside of Curtis, she could hear his silly laugh inside himself knowing he had scared them by shaking the tall grass behind them.

It made her smile that he had let his guard down long enough to let her see in. She loved those moments when she could read him, when he was fresh and himself. When he wasn't hiding from her.

Curtis stood to his full height behind Shelley. "Family meeting?" he questioned them with a chuckle.

Jordy turned his head with his body still sitting on the chair. "Something like that." He told Curtis behind him. He was still truly shaken by the fact that Curtis had came upon them without notice. He made a mental note to explore that thought with Shelley later.

Curtis looked back and forth at the two of them. He sat down in the chair next to Shelley. "I'm not sure if the great goddess here has explained my mere, useless abilities to you or not, but I wasn't blessed with the damn gift of reading minds like you all are. Care to fill me in Jordy?"

Shelley felt the hit against her soul like a slap. The way Curtis could talk always had her in a tizzy. He always seemed to point his anger right her.

Jordy noticed it as well. Curtis was different now. His hatred was overpowering him. He made a mental note to explore that later also. For now, Curtis needed to know their plan.

"As I am sure you already know, your brother Asher and Emie have been split up and Emie has been missing for some time."

"If you are here to get my advice like your brother Jeremy did in hopes of me helping her, I can't help you." Curtis had no intentions of helping them. He couldn't stand to look at his family because of the beast he had become. He was not going to go and talk to Asher or Emie now.

He still blamed Shelley for that. Curtis looked down at his own knees and rubbed them hard with his hands. His new skin still itched from the healing. But he was no longer scarred like he had been.

Shelley took note of that. Curtis had not sat still long enough for her to read him. To understand why he had so much hatred in his heart for her. It was only of late that he felt this way. She looked at Jordy in hopes he had learned anything. He only nodded at her and whispered in her mind he would help with that later.

"You've been listening to the news, I hope?" Jordy questioned him, hoping the change in topic might sway his decision.

"No not really. Have I missed something?"

Jordy almost chuckled at his brashness. Only the destruction of cities around the world, he wanted to say.

"There is a war upon us Curtis. One that this family has been aware of for some time now. You were chosen by us, and by God, to assist us in this fight. For the protection of as much as we can handle."

Curtis looked at Shelley then for confirmation. When she nodded her head at him, he cussed aloud.

"Well, I'll be damned." He had heard somewhat of Jordy was saying on the televisions at the bars he had been visiting.

Jordy shook that one off. That was not the way he would have put it. "Nevertheless, it is your family that needs you now."

Curtis swung his head so sharply at Jordy that Shelley shivered. Every move he made caused her to quiver in some form or another.

She wished he would understand though. She hadn't meant to damn him.

Jordy took note of all Shelley's thought. He was needed here more than he had first thought. He knew he was not much of the match maker, that was clear with how well he had done with Emie and Asher, but he was going to try with Shelley and Curtis.

"We are not the demons here Curtis."

"Then what are we Jordy? Please, forgive me if I don't buy into this angelic bull shit you all keep telling me I am. We are vampires! Just like what is out there now destroying this world. And I am going nowhere near my family as long as I can help it!"

Curtis said as he stood to shake off the rage he felt. He looked down at his arms then. He needed to feed again.

"Curtis, sit down!"

This commanding voice from behind them all made them turn around. It was Joseph. His eyes were all on Curtis. Commanding. Domineering. Full of power.

Jordy smiled then. Joseph had the ability to cower even the strongest of men and vampires. He was grateful he was here. Curtis wasn't one to bow out of a fight, but bow out he would do for Joseph.

Joseph nodded to Shelley as he approached her. Curtis had sat immediately at his command. It seemed that all Joseph had done in the beginning of Curtis' training had worked. Curtis feared him, and that was just fine with Joseph.

But now it was time for Curtis to listen.

Joseph stood off to the side of them all. He looked out onto the ocean in front of them all. He hated this, he thought to himself with a deep inhale of the ocean breeze.

He had lost his little sister to Curtis' little stubborn brother Asher, and he hated them both for it. Now that he knew she was safe and would be coming home soon, he wanted to gather his whole family together for her homecoming. Even if it killed him to be under one roof with Curtis and Asher. He would deal with Asher later for what he had done to Emie, in his own way.

"Curtis, you have to listen to us. Once and for all." He said to Curtis looking toward him, but not at him. "You were not created by us or by Shelley, you were chosen. You are not the vampire Hollywood or any story teller with a wit about him has portrayed you to be."

He looked behind him, straight at Curtis then. "The sooner you accept this, the sooner we can move on."

Curtis sighed, deeply. He let his head fall into his hands. Joseph's will, could be felt in every fiber of his body. His will was powerful, and Curtis knew he would need to either bend to it or break.

Curtis could hear Shelley in his mind and all his memories of her, they were all dancing around like a movie in slow motion. He could see their wings in his mind, all of which made them who they were. Angelic. The tender hearted compassionate family that they were stood them apart from what he so brazenly believed them to be.

Joseph was right about Hollywood. But Curtis still had so many questions about everything.

When he finally lifted his head to look at them all, each one looked pleased with his decision, and it only ate him up inside.

Jordy was the first to speak then. "Your family needs you Curtis. More than we do. Asher needs you back in his life. And you have a nephew, Darryl. In a year-"

"What about Darryl?" Curtis questioned him standing to his full height. Darryl was more than just his nephew to him. He was one of his best friends. Or had been, he thought off handedly.

Jordy looked at him more directly. "Darryl is going to need our help in a few months. I can't tell you more than that," he said to him trying to get him to sit back down. "Listen, Curtis-"

"No Jordy! Tell me!" Curtis fumed, wanting to know more.

Jordy took a deep breath then and looked at Joseph for help.

Curtis almost sat back down then. Frightened by what Joseph might do to him for his outburst. But he stood his ground. He had to know what Jordy was talking about.

Joseph looked at Curtis exasperated. He walked up to Curtis and put his hand on his shoulder. It was just easier this way.

Shelley had to look away. It hurt to watch as Curtis went down to one knee. She could see what Joseph was doing to his mind and knew it was painful. But it needed to be done. Curtis would have to listen now.

Joseph showed Curtis everything. Every damn thing the fool was too prideful to listen too. He may have been one of the best and hardest working firefighters this world had ever seen, and he may hate them for what they had done to him, even though his life had already been over, but to Joseph, he knew Curtis could be the man he once was again. Even if he had to make him that way.

Joseph showed Curtis everything. From the beginning of creation and how they all had come into existence, to the fall of the evil ones on this Earth that had been destroying this world a hundred times over. He showed him why in the last century men had prospered. It wasn't for the good of man. It was because the evil ones were allowing it and helping to fulfill their master plan.

There was a great apocalypse coming. A judgment of this dying world.

He showed Curtis what they really were, who they were, everything and all his family had done, and why. Starting with his sister Emie and how she had been turned by the worst demon of all. How her beautiful life had been ended and destroyed by him. How he sought to destroy her still.

He showed him how Asher and Curtis himself, now that he was one of them, fit into their master plan. And in exchange for their help, Joseph vowed to protect their family and friends in return. It was what he had been doing all along. What he intended to do, with or without their help. But Joseph needed them. He made of point of showing that to Curtis too.

"As for your nephew," Joseph told him, letting go of him and giving him a moment to hear him now. "He is in the special forces unit of the Army."

Curtis rubbed his head. "Yes. Intel."

"He is out there right now secretly fighting for the Army against those demons I showed you. The evil ones who are out there secretly destroying kingdoms, and governments, cities and families. I don't have all the answers yet, nor do I know his whereabouts. All I can tell you is that in a year from now, he is going to come to us and need our help. But we are going to need him more. And he won't help us without you." Joseph let that sink in through his thick skull.

"Do you understand? He is trained to kill us, destroy us, because he, like you, doesn't understand the difference between us and the evil ones. He is a greater force against us than the evil ones. But if he sees you, or Asher, he will stop, and hopefully listen to me."

Curtis looked at Joseph now. He understood. That much he was sure of. He could see the plan Shelley had been trying to tell him about now. He looked at her too now. For the first time, he really looked at her. The way she smiled at him and turned away broke his heart. He had said and done cruel things to her he regretted now.

Curtis looked at Joseph. "Just tell me what you want me to do."

Joseph nodded at Jordy who was smiling now. They had finally gotten through.

Joseph looked more pointedly at Curtis. "You had better get that disappearing act under control before I break your legs. And you owe her an apology." He said looking tenderly over at Shelley, and then back at Curtis. "If I ever have to come down here again because you have hurt her, I swear I will leave you with only a torso attached to that pretty little head of yours."

Curtis looked at Shelley then. "Can he do that?" This bit of information was new to him.

Shelley smiled at Joseph. The threat was more of a strike of fear cast at Curtis. One that was pointedly accepted. Joseph was harmless though, she thought with a smile of her own. And even though she was the only one who knew this, she let Curtis believe it.

She turned slowly to Curtis and smiled. All her threats in training him had never worked on him before because he knew he could escape her grasp by disappearing. It had been a game to him.

"Oh yes. And when he leaves you to me," She leaned in closer to make her point. "Just think of all the things; wonderful, gruesome things I will do to you. That is what you should really be afraid of!"

Curtis sat back in the sand and huffed. He looked at them more clearly though now. They were family. And now he was their family.

June 2016
Six months later…

Curtis had spent time with Asher in the Whitby home after he and Emie had happily reunited. He had been glad to finally see his brother again, and had surprised even himself with his strengths. Curtis had worried over nothing thinking he would attack his brother like some grueling vampire.

He wasn't a vampire he reminded himself, looking over the moonlit ocean. He was an angel. And now Asher knew it too. They weren't the vampires who were destroying everything. Not the vampires everyone feared in their nightmares.

Curtis was sitting out on the shore by Shelley's house. By their house, he corrected himself. He sighed at that and smiled.

Shelley was adorable to him. He didn't understand why he'd never seen it before but she was funny and witty. She was brilliant, and beautiful. She drove him mad with her beauty, but he would never let her see it.

He had never met anyone like her he thought to himself. From her lovely, rich red, spiral hair he loved to watch her play with, to her lips he couldn't seem to stop looking at; he realized some time ago that he was falling for her.

His heart still ached when he thought about what she had done to him though. How she had fooled his family on his deathbed and walked out of the hospital with his burnt body. And then how she had turned him without even asking his permission.

He had to admit now, that he understood why she had done it, but he still didn't like the way they had done it. Angels or not, they had been wrong about him and Asher.

He wondered then about Asher. If Emie and Joseph had come to them earlier, before he had gone on that call that night, would he and Asher have listened to the Whitby's and their plans for their lives?

"Maybe, but then there's the whole romantic love story of it all." Shelley winked at him from off in the distance. She had been swimming out there with the manatees when she heard his thoughts about Emie and Asher.

As much as he hated when she did that, listening into his thoughts, she had caught his attention, and he had to know more. "Romantic?" He asked as he got up from his chair and disappeared.

Shelley gasped the moment she found herself wrapped up in Curtis' strong arms. She would never get used to it, she told herself. He had mastered his disappearing act, she told herself. Even she was amazed at it.

She looked down at his bare chest, dripping with ocean water and closed her eyes and whispered aloud "Yes." Half scared to death in the arms of this man. When she opened them again, she noticed what Emie had told her. Curtis was staring at her lips!

"Why don't you tell me about it, darlin'?" Curtis smiled at her, pulling her closer to him. He stilled owed her that apology, but he was hell bound on making her deserve it first.

Shelley bit her lip. Where did she begin in the telling of Emie's love story?

"One night, when you and Asher were out playing by the canals with your friends, you had to have been ten or eleven then I think." She told him as she thought about it. "Emie had just come home from work and was headed out to the beach. She could hear the teasing going on between all of you. Picking on poor Asher." She eyed him shamefully, tisking at him.

Curtis remembered it. All the stories they had told about the Whitby family behind their stone walls and gated property. All the kids had everyone in town believing there were vampires and werewolf living there. They had gotten it all wrong though.

"Vampires, not so much. Werewolf's, yes." She thought off handedly looking away from Curtis sheepishly.

"Seriously? That's what those servants are?" Curtis asked her, asking about the servants at the Whitby's home.

"Now do you want to hear this story or not?" She eyed him curiously again, winking at him. Doing so caused her to look into his eyes more closely. Oh, his eyes, she thought. They were grey when he was angry and hungry, they were a bright red when he was content and full, and almost violet, a mixture of red and blue, when he was acting almost human, almost like himself, Shelley thought pensively.

He relented, still curious she noticed, and so she continued. "When Emie felt for young Asher on the other side of the walls, she could feel his unease. She could feel how mean all you brats were being to him." She teased Curtis. "Emie came up to the wall and listened into his heart and mind and smiled. He couldn't see her of course, and neither could she him. But she knew who he was."

"She had known about him since the night he was born in the hospital." Shelley remembered thoughtfully. Emie had been working the night Asher had been born. "She had been working there that night, you see, when he was born." Shelley closed her eyes at the memories. "Emie had to draw blood on Asher the night he was born. I remember her telling me of the beautiful baby boy she had seen that night." Shelley bit her lip remembering it all. Shelley had known about this whole love story even then.

"Anyways, that night out by the wall, Emie whispered to Asher's heart."

Curtis waited for her to say what Emie had said to his brother. "Well? What did she say to him?" He said aloud getting her out of her head.

"You have to promise me you won't ever tell him this?" Hoping Curtis never would reveal this one secret.

Curtis eyed her curiously.

"Emie will have my head." She explained. "She whispered to his heart a curiosity. She wanted him to never be afraid of her. And she wanted him to be so curious that one day he would come and find her."

"You see, Emie knew then the kind of man Asher was. Who he would become. She knew him inside. Unlike anyone else ever would. She didn't know then that she would fall helplessly and hopelessly in love with him the way she did, but we all knew. It was something all of us seers had to wait for."

Curtis looked at her lips as she spoke to him. How could he not?

He would find a way to tease his brother about it all someday, and he had to admit it was very romantic and all. But Shelley was in his arms now. Her legs were dangling around him. When she took a deep breath, he knew she could hear his thoughts.

He let her go then though. Wretched heart of his that it was, he wondered something he needed answers too. "Did you know about me? Before Joseph came to you and told you his plans." If she said yes, it could change everything for him. He didn't understand it, but he felt it somewhere deep inside of soul.

Shelley wanted to tell him yes. She could see the romantic idea he had now stuck in his jealous head. Their story wasn't like that though. She had been with many men before him. She loved, and she had lost more than she cared to remember.

When she had heard Emie telling the story of how Curtis had given his life in a heroic measure to save his brother's life a year ago, and the fact that she was attracted to men in uniform, she had vainly jumped at the chance to be the one who got to turn him, not really knowing what she was getting herself into.

She had never seen that she would have fallen for him the way she had though. She would never understand that either.

She looked at Curtis then and could see what Jordy was talking about. She was in love with him.

But he was not in love with her. Even though he was trying.

"Never mind." Curtis said as he disappeared from her.

Shelley wrapped her arms around herself and wept. It was her own personal, tragic, love story. She was no poet, and would never understand why he hated her so much. But Curtis would never understand her feelings either, because he was always so busy running away from his own. He couldn't hear or feel any of them, because he wouldn't let himself do it.

Chapter Six: New Mission

Ellis Island
January 2017, one year later…

Darryl's team had lost contact with Intel in July. By August they had lost contact with everyone.

Slowly, everything known to man had been demolished and destroyed. Cities, towns, people and animals alike had been torn apart. When the lights went out around the world, in one night of one day, everything was broken and on fire. Swarms of vampiric armies took over the Earth in a swift sweep that ravaged civilization as it was known to man.

It had happened slowly over the last year. In the beginning, Darryl had noticed the strategic plan of the enemy, the deaths of many very important Intel members along with a very big portion of the United States government. There were more reports of top secret officials dying or disappearing as the year went on. Every one Darryl was fighting for, were gone. It was very well thought out and strategic the way this enemy moved; Darryl had been very impressed by it.

When the White House got over run by what the news had reported as terrorist, Darryl and his men knew the United States was lost to the enemy. Once the US and its military fell, all the kingdoms and governments around the world fell also.

No one had seen it coming. Except for Darryl.

His team, in a last effort to finish their mission even though they had no one to repot it too, had taken them months to do it. They had secured Ellis Island in a few day's time once they had reached it. They had killed many demonic looking creatures upon entering New York City, like they had entered a new realm in the world. They took over a museum there on the island, but then unease set in unlike any time before.

What now? It was question on all the men's minds. And Darryl felt just as helpless.

Across from the island, stood the trade tower that they were to seek out and investigate. Two vampires from the house of Victor, the world's most feared vampire, had taken over the tower there and set up Victor's main central center.

One of Darryl's men had died that day Darryl had taken the island. Toby. His death hit Darryl harder than any before him. Toby was young and full of life…

Darryl started to question God again over his death, but he never got the answers he was looking for.

What their mission had entailed was that the trade center tower had been overtaken by Victor's army. It was being secured by Axel and another vampire Darryl didn't know. And Darryl would now have to figure out what to do on his own about it, with only Bartley, Jimmy, Johnny and Patrick to help him. Instead of the hundreds that were supposed to meet him here and fight alongside him.

Darryl was not only feeling defeated tonight, their third night on the island, but he was also weary. He had chosen the Ellis Island because it was the best vantage point to see the trade tower across the bay from where they were without getting too close to the enemy. It was also the one place the monsters hadn't over taken yet.

He found himself asking haunting questions again: why. He still didn't understand God's reasons. He honestly didn't think he ever would. He was even starting to wonder if there was a God anymore after all he had witnessed.

Darryl was looking out at the endless midnight skyline above him through the skylight windows in the museum. As sweat and dirt he wiped from his head drenched him on the bitterly cold night, he tried to find reasons for it all. He closed his eyes and remembered all the death and destruction he had witnessed these last few months as his homeland had fallen to one of the worst swarms of demonic power he had ever seen.

If God did exist, he was cruel, in his own mind, Darryl thought to himself, trying to close his weary eyes.

His men were all around him, trying to sleep also. It had been days since they had slept for more than a few moments. The dogs had even passed out, weary and unable to keep guard any more.

Tonight, in the midnight hours, in the museum that held more history than any other of its kind, all they wanted to do was sleep, and protect themselves the best they could. There was nowhere else to run too.

Nothing else was left.

He couldn't speak for his own family and friends at home, but he was sure from the destruction he had seen in their travels here, that they were lost too. He looked at his men and wondered about their families also.

He thought of Asher then as he rested his back more up against the wall, trying to find a comfortable position. Asher had promised him he would keep their family safe.

Darryl shook his head of the endless pictures his mind had taken while out hunting down the enemy. There was no way Asher would have been able to keep anyone safe let alone himself. Darryl let that sink in, and then he mourned his family and friends in the night around him.

While sitting on main floor of the museum, Darryl was searching for answers. He remembered Ken then. Talia's brother. He had told Darryl that if he asked God anything, God would answer him.

Darryl asked God then, in the darkness of the night that was falling around him as he looked up into the starry night, he called out to Him in a whisper. He had to know why.

"Just tell me why-"

No, he told himself. He wanted another answer if he was going to get any.

And then there it was again. That feeling he hadn't felt in over a year. He could feel her again. When he looked at his scarred hand that was lying on top of his weapon he could swear he could feel her hand there on his.

"Why did you have to take her from me?" Darryl whispered looking down at her hand he knew wasn't there.

It was the second time he had ever asked God anything, and he wasn't expecting an answer. But if he got anything from God, he wanted it to be this.

Out of nowhere, the glass windows above him broke. Glass was raining down on him and his men, like thunder breaking the silence of a peaceful night before a storm. They all bolted up out of a sleepy haze, stood their ground and fought the demons that were floating down above them trying to kill them.

Again.

Darryl ducked under one of them as it flew past him and he was knocked off his feet and flung across the room. He hit his back and head on the floor behind him and lost all sense of direction.

A pain in his back, a pain he hadn't felt in years, racked through his spine and brought him back to his senses.

It wasn't until he came to and he could see his men were standing around him awe struck that he realized someone, or something was on top of him. When he looked at the 'something' in question, all he could see was white ash and blue sparkling feathers covering his lower body.

But there in his arms, holding on to him for dear life, was the body of an angel, blonde curls swirling all around her.

More demons came through the broken windows. His men stood guard over him, but they were scattered, and Darryl had to pick himself and the angel up. He threw his weapon over his shoulder as he stood with her in his arms and carried her back to the wall, under the stairs that led to the upper floors, where he knew there was a room that led beneath the stairs.

He walked until he found it, breaking his back worse than before from carrying the helpless body. Once inside, out of exhaustion from the pain in his back he had to lower himself and sit against the door and brace himself against it with her in his arms.

Her? He questioned himself as he looked down at the angel in his arms.

It really was an angel in his arms he noticed, stunned into silence.

Like waves of thunder, the war raged on behind him. His men, tired and war weary, fought harder than they had before, while Darryl sat staring dumbfounded at the angel in his arms that seemed more like a dream then reality.

The room was dark. Windows around him let in a little moon light, just enough that he could make out what he was holding unto. When reality hit him, he wondered if it was possible that he had just hit his head harder than he had thought and he was still unconscious out there with his men instead of in here, holding an angel in his arms.

He tried to blow her feathers out of his face, and realized then he wasn't dreaming. He could feel everything around him; the cold icy bite of the night, the cold sweat dripping down his forehead that her feathers were sticking too, and then there was reality of her in his arms. He could feel her form, her body, the length and glow of her hair and wings. It was so surreal to him in that moment.

White, ashy, bluish glossy feathers stretched out over his left side, wrapped around her and him like her wing was gathered around him holding unto him. It was the most sensual thing he had ever witnessed in his life, the way she was holding onto him. Her arms were tucked neatly in-between them. She was grabbing onto his vest with one hand and the other was softly pressed on his chest.

Darryl tried to move her lovely feathers that were covering her head. Her head was full of blonde curls and she smelled just as heavenly as she looked, but he noticed her hair was stained with blood and it coated her back and feathers in splatters.

He couldn't see her face as he moved her sweet hair out of his way with his fingers. Her face was tucked down in his chest. She was unconscious, or so he thought, and bleeding, a lot. Darryl searched her body then for the wound he knew was there.

It was her other wing, that was straining to lift up he noticed; it had been cut clean to the bone, off. What he thought was blood was pouring out of the wound with every painful movement it made.

Slowly, years of training took over his mind, without a thought he pulled off his vest that held a supply of things he needed on nights like tonight, and pulled out of one of the pockets bandages. He wrapped what he could of her wing where the bone had been severed to stop the bleeding. He had no idea what he was doing; only that he knew he had to stop the bleeding, angel or not. When he was finished, he was grateful she had slept through the worst of it.

When he had her wing bandaged up the best he could, blowing more feathers out of his sweat soaked, bloody face that was smeared with blood from her wounds, he lifted her face and tried to get her to look at him.

Darryl started to plea with her as he tried to tip up her face. Tried to talk to her, tried to wake her. When her head finally lifted up and fell back, he stroked her face trying to understand who... what was she? He wondered looking lovingly into the face of the angel.

Angels weren't real... were they? Well, he thought with a laugh, ten years ago neither were vampires or demons.

And then, that feeling was there again. That chill he hated that would consume his body. But when he really looked at her, with unknowing feelings that raged within him, he knew what that was.

Talia.

Darryl lost all thought as he looked into her face and she slowly opened her void less, black eyes. His breathing stopped, then it quickened. And then he understood that wonderful, terrible feeling. It was that same feeling he had always gotten when he was with her. She gave him chills. He knew it and he recognized it, remembering it from years past when he was with her.

She had never left him, even in death.

He couldn't think then. All he could see was her face.

She had the face of a goddess. An angel, he corrected himself. Beautiful just didn't cover it. She was so much more than that though. But he was sure, more than positive; it was Talia's face he was looking into.

Darryl stared in disbelief at her face. He looked her over again just to make sure he hadn't been dreaming about her wings. Was she truly an angel?

She was broken, injured, but she was alive, and she was an angel! And somehow, though he couldn't explain it, she was in his arms.

Everything stopped. Completely froze for him.

With the world around him completely forgotten, a blinding light washed the room, and real thunder roared in his ears. In the midst of the light, a man stood, and for the first time in a long time, Darryl was afraid.

His gun was lodged somewhere behind his back and he knew he was completely defenseless. There was absolutely nothing he could do in those timeless moments.

A paralytic feeling washed throughout his body and he couldn't move a muscle in his body. He couldn't even look up at the man who was standing before him.

Darryl feared even the smallest of movements, wishing he could cover his eyes from the blinding light in front of him. All he could do was try to hug Talia close to his body and try to protect her.

He waited for death, but it never came. In the quiet that filled the room, in a stillness that awed him, a voice filled the room.

"My name is Gabriel."

Knowledge. Wisdom that Darryl had never felt before, over took his soul and he knew the person wasn't a man, it was an angel standing before him.

"The angel in your arms, her name is Vestalia."

"Vestalia is the dew from heaven, an angel made in the creation of time, who had been created to live, exists for one purpose. For a reason only God knows."

"And herein lies her mystery; she was placed into the womb of a human to be reborn into the world as Talia Kruse, the woman you would fall in love with, and the woman who would love you above anything else in this world, so that she, and she alone, could protect you and love you with a selfless, powerful, death defying love that would never dissipate or cease to exist. A love that was not only created in heaven and blessed by God himself, but was formed in your own hearts equally, held onto tightly, molded and sculpted into your souls, felt stirringly throughout your bodies, and will be cherished throughout eternity by the two of you. For your love defined not only the meaning of love, but it defied the foundations, the boundaries of what was believed enough."

"In your love, there is no end, just the beginning of a beautiful love story." The angel whispered astonished.

"God gave you this." He finished.

Darryl couldn't believe the divinity of it all. He wanted to weep like a child. There were no words to explain it all. He only felt shame. Shame in himself for the coward he had been in the face of God. He had known all along God existed; he just hadn't wanted to admit it.

He had shamefully needed someone to blame for her death, and he had sinfully blamed the God who had blessed him with something so amazing.

He knew now and believed what everyone had tried to tell him. God did have a reason and a purpose. And he didn't deserve to know what it was now.

He held onto Talia, the girl he had loved as a child, and the one he now had loved his whole adult life. She had been his angel. She had given her life for him out of love, yes, but also because it was what she was meant to do. Protect him.

She was his angel! The reality of it hit harder than the blow that had knocked him down earlier.

This, her; she was his answer.

A man, or what Darryl thought was a man, was kneeling before him now. A different man, Darryl could sense. Darryl didn't know who it was, but it was no longer the angel who had been standing before him.

Darryl feared whoever it was would take Talia from him, so he held her tighter.

Darryl feared it was God himself. And when he spoke, Darryl knew it was Him.

"I am." He said to Darryl in a stillness that shook him.

It was Him, and Darryl knew he didn't deserve whatever it was he was being blessed with.

"If you are going to take my life because of what I have done," Darryl begged looking at his broken angel. "Just save hers please!"

He held her tighter then and remembered her beauty that had nothing to do with her body. Talia had an inner beauty that deserved a better life than the one he had given her. She deserved so much more out of life then being stuck by his side and struck down again. Somehow, he knew she had done it again. She had saved his life again tonight.

Darryl wanted to look and plead with God. He wanted to beg for her life. He hated he had done this to her.

"Darryl, my son, please listen to me. I have a plan. My will, will be done this night. This war will be over soon. I will avenge my people. My protectors. My creation. But I need your help."

"I need a hero."

Shame filled Darryl like never before. Darryl knew he couldn't look up in the face of God. He kept his sinful head bowed and asked, "What can I do?"

Darryl felt God's smile. In that moment, he knew he was saved from whatever fate he had damned his own soul with. He had never believed in God before. And now here He was. Saving him like the savior He was.

"Take her home, Darryl."

Darryl heard the whisper of God, but he felt it more. He felt it in his own soul.

Home...

Darryl squeezed his eyes shut tighter as the tears fell from his cheeks and he remembered home. He wanted to go home so bad.

Then God's words hit him like a rock. He could take Talia home. With him!

Darryl's eye opened wide and he looked at her then. He tipped her face so he could look at her. Her eyes weren't open like before, but she was there, with him, and he could take her home with him. It was all he had ever wanted.

Darryl watched as a hand stroked the hair of Talia's head. There, in the midst of His hands, Darryl saw the unmistakable mark of his savior. The nail prints that told the story of His love.

"Your Uncle Asher is there. He has kept his promise to you."

More tears fell unto Darryl's lips as he listened to the words of God. His mouth was dripping, watering. Asher, his uncle, was still alive. Darryl didn't know how Asher had done it, but in that moment, he couldn't wait to see Asher again. And his family.

"Asher will tell you everything you need to know. And she will be yours. She is all you ever wanted and asked for from me. This I promise to you, she is yours now."

Darryl listened with a heavy heart as his savior stood up and he watched as the white shining robe swirled around His bare feet. Darryl could see the perfect impressions of the scars on His feet. For the first time ever, Darryl thought about the pain this man must have went through in those moments of His death. The pain He had endured for someone as stubborn and sinful as him. Darryl knew he didn't deserve the angel in his arms, or the savior standing before him. They had both risked, and broken their lives for him.

Darryl could hear the perfect sigh of God, and in that moment, he felt God's perfect, unfailing love for his wretched soul. He knew then, God's love had nothing to do with what he had been or done in life, but rather who Darryl was. Darryl was a child of God, and like the parental love a father bestows on his child. God loved Darryl with the greatest unwavering love in existence.

Darryl listened to the words God spoke to him.

"She's been fighting for you. Day after day she's been struggling trying to protect you since the day she fell in love with you. Because she loved you so much I allowed her to be the guardian by your side. But this war is bigger than her now. Now she needs you to protect her.

"See to her wounds Darryl. Your love for her will heal her, like the love of my children has healed mine. No one will ever hurt her again."

And with that last whisper, He was gone.

Darryl stayed like that for hours. Mystified. Holding onto Talia for his life in the darkness. He didn't understand, he couldn't explain it. But there it was, here she was, in his arms, holding unto him too.

When he could no longer hear the fight outside the door, he worried about his men. But for whatever reason he felt compelled to hide in here with her. To protect her. Something had wounded her, it might even still be looking for her, and he didn't want anything else to happen to her, ever again.

The Angel in Darryl's arms was indeed the woman he had loved his entire life. She stirred alive with rushing feelings. Memories filled her mind and fluttered through her heart like butterflies. For the first time in years she felt the awakening reviving her soul. She was still the angel she had been. But somehow, now she was becoming the woman again she had once been.

Talia, still dizzy from the extreme pain she felt and the confusion of where she was, came to and looked up into the eyes of the man she had loved her entire life. The man she had spent the past years protecting as his guardian angel because she had given her life selflessly for him and refused to leave his side, ever. She was looking up into his eyes, and by some power she didn't understand, he was looking back into hers.

She blinked many times trying to understand it. She wasn't supposed to be here like this. She had wished it so many times, yes, but had she finally willed it into existence with a power she didn't know she had, she questioned herself.

The pull of the pain was so heavy she couldn't concentrate on anything any longer.

Trying to hold onto reality, she wrapped her arms around him and lazily let the haze of this nightmare take hold of her mind. She hadn't felt pain since the night she had died so many years ago as a human.

Willing her mind not to let go, to hold onto him just a little longer, was like a heaven she was willing to accept.

She tried to remember in those moments what had happened just moments ago out there while she inhaled the scent of Darryl. She had been back to back with Darryl, ready to fight off any demon that tried to attack him. She had been ready for it when she heard the screeching of a demon coming at Darryl from above. She had left his back for only a moment when he had been knocked down and thrown by another demon, but then something had hit her back and everything went black.

Talia sighed. She didn't know what was happening. Maybe this was her final death. Maybe this was God's way of giving her one last moment in the only heaven she had ever wanted. She opened her eyes once more and tried to accept the gift she thought she was being given.

Darryl noticed her eyes, black as the night around him, opened again. Darryl held his breath as her long lashes that moments ago had been resting peacefully against her cheek now fluttered open. She stirred in pain and buried her face in his arms. He hushed her and started talking to her again.

"Talia. You are safe now, I promise." He whispered to her holding her head against his chest. He stroked her hair in disbelief. He was choking on his own words, but he couldn't seem to stop them as he spoke to her more trying to get her attention.

Even though it was reality he felt with her, he still couldn't believe it. He was smiling, shaking his head in laughter, and his heart was breaking at it all at the same time.

He looked down at her thin clothing and seen the white robe she was wearing. The silkiness of it he felt on his arm that was holding her felt softer than anything he had ever felt before. He had never felt anything like it so soft. She truly was an angel, he thought to himself. His angel.

He had caught her in his arms during the fight. She must have fallen onto him trying to protect him again. She had to have been fighting with him, he told himself. And that damn demon had cut her and strike her down. He looked down at her and reasoned with himself all the ways he was going to tell her she had to stop doing that. He couldn't ever lose her again, he thought as he moved her hair away from her face.

Darryl looked at her through frightened eyes now. She was a fighter; she always had been for him when they were younger. She had always had his back, and had never left side. Now, he understood why.

When she looked up into his eyes, with her black eyes, Darryl was frightened more. He tried to think of what he should be doing, where he should be, but nothing else mattered right now, but her. When she closed her eyes again her head fell back on his arm and he tried to hold her, to steady her.

He sighed greatly trying to understand that. She must be in extreme pain if she was still falling into unconsciousness.

He had been fighting demons out there, but he hadn't a clue that angels had been fighting with him. That she, the woman he had loved for so long, had been beside him all along, fighting with him. And now, as he looked at her broken wing, he hated the demons with a fierceness stronger than before.

Talia didn't know what was going on. Every time she came to, she ran through Darryl's mind and found the information she needed. She had been fighting off that demon, and of course he hadn't seen her. He wasn't supposed to. So why could he see her now?

It had to have been the demon, she told herself, as she drifted out again. He must have done this to her when he had struck her down. She could feel the pain in her back and wing. But she couldn't hold onto to reality enough to understand it.

She shouldn't be here in his arms like she was...

Her mind lost track for what felt like hours. She felt like she was floating in the clouds. Memories of who she was filled her mind and mixed with thoughts of who she had been to him. Who Darryl was to her. He was her love, her life. She was sworn to protect him. Keep him safe. He was hers.

For the first time in what felt like forever, she felt the stirring of what those thoughts caused. She could feel the stirring of butterflies and it made it her soul smile.

Talia looked at him then, she willed the power she still felt in her soul to keep her awake for longer than a blink of an eye this time.

Darryl watched her try to open her eyes like she had heard his thoughts about the demon, when suddenly she sweetly reached up and touched his face. Suddenly his mind was filled with memories of him fighting. Like a drug, he tried to shake it off, but couldn't. He placed his hand on hers while she showed him she had been there beside him all along. She showed him where she had been, and how she had tried to save him.

"I know Talia. I know." He told her. Her touch was so soft. Her hand in his he squeezed. He'd never felt hands so baby soft as hers before.

He had to know more.

The angel in his arms looked at him astonished. She showed him more, years where she had been with him. By his side as his angel.

Memories for him filled his mind. And with every memory he felt that feeling. That feeling he thought he hated. But it was her that his body had responded to. She showed him how she had done it. How she had moved through his body and stirred him.

The last memory he seen was the one where he was standing at her grave not so long ago. She was trying to show him she had been there with him standing behind him with her arms around him. Darryl shook his head no as the memory disappeared and her hand fell along with her head again. She closed her eyes again and the images stopped, and he found himself lost in her thoughts. She had left him with so many pieces of his own past he didn't know what to do with them all.

She had showed him so much, but not enough. He wanted to wake her up, but he could see how much pain she was in. Anything she did, from moving, to blinking, and trying to concentrate took so much out of her. Using her powers to speak to him must have been too much for her.

What was he supposed to do now? His men needed him, but he couldn't just leave her here, he thought as he hit his head back against the door. He looked down at her again. She was his angel; she had been trying to save him his whole life. He hadn't even known she was there all along.

But now he did… and he refused to let her go. He refused to leave her.

He held her until his arms gave out and his back felt like it was in flames, and then he held her longer. It wasn't until the dawn peaked through the windows above him that she stirred.

He stirred awake when she did. He even pulled her into him more so she couldn't get away.

She looked up and he looked down at her.

"Well, hello there again." He grinned.

Talia smiled shyly and looked back down. She thought she had been dreaming, but she hadn't. This was new, yes, but it was real, she thought offhandedly with a grin of her own.

Darryl smiled wider then. She always had done that to him in the past. He would smile at her, and she would smile and blush and look away. He loved it then, and he loved it even more now.

Love. He remembered what God had said. His love would heal her, he told himself as he moved a stray feather off her tender face. Darryl didn't know if it was possible, but he let his love for her live again in his heart. She was here, right here in his arms he told himself as he looked her over from her gorgeous hair to her beautiful bare feet. He could feel the power of it growing inside himself, and it made him smile. He would use it as often as he could, whatever it took to heal her, to keep her alive.

Talia hissed at the sunlight that was creeping up to her bare toes from the windows above them and crawled away from him into the corner.

Darryl watched her move in pain. He was surprised she had gotten off him, but the emptiness he felt without her in his arms worried him.

"Hey, your safe." He told her as he followed her with his arm. She was right next to him, but not close enough. She looked like she was in pain as he watched her feel for her damaged wing.

Talia bent her head trying to think and tried to find the source of her pain as she reached behind her. Her entire wing was gone, and what was left was damaged, broken, she thought. The thought of it made her eyes water and tears spilled from them.

She couldn't stand on her feet either. She was an angel, and angels didn't feel pain nor did they have to stand. Talia placed her hands on the floor in front of her and tried to grasp reality.

Darryl, she thought, openly as she looked over at him. He wasn't supposed to see her; he wasn't supposed to know she existed. But there, her gentle giant was. Over there, right next to her looking at her like he was.

"I did my best trying to bandage your… wing." He told her astonished by the idea of her having wings. Beautiful wings, lined with soft, glossy feathers, he thought more to himself without being able to form the words.

When she looked straight at him, she had to shake her head and understand what was going on. But nothing made sense as she looked around the room where they were. Even his thoughts and words were like clouds to her. She couldn't see through them. All she could do was lower her head to the floor and pray she didn't die yet.

Darryl watched as she lowered her head and wished she would talk to him. But then, she looked at him sideways rolling her precious head toward him, and he was sure she could read his thoughts right then and there. He smiled at her then and let her know he understood.

Talia looked at Darryl. Her heart tugged at him. She wanted to speak to him. She needed to tell him what was happening, where he was supposed to be. But in that moment, she didn't care about duty or reasons anymore and she didn't want him to leave her. She vainly only cared that he could see her now. That all she had to do was reach out and she could touch him. Something she had not been able to do in so long.

The pain made her lay down though. She couldn't bear it anymore. Her back and what was left of her wing ached in stabbing pain.

When his thoughts entered her mind as she turned her head back down, she knew she needed to tell him who she was. But she couldn't. She was bound by her secrets also. He wouldn't be able to withstand the power of her voice. No human could.

"Hey." Darryl said to her as he inched closer over to her the best he could. He could see she was in pain, and he wanted her to know she didn't have to bare it alone.

"Come here. You're safe now." He said to her again. Once he was out of the sun light like she was, he watched as she curled up half on his lap and he let her. It was the sexiest thing he had ever witnessed the way she pulled her body off the ground and found his legs and curled her body into his, folding her wing around them like she had before.

Darryl watched her wing as it did like it had a mind of its own. The thought made his heart dance.

Her wing was so beautiful. He watched as the air moved and rustled the soft feathers, as every breath she took moved them also.

Darryl looked back down at his angel, at Talia. She was so brave...

Love, he reminded himself. Love her Darryl, he told himself.

He could really see her, she thought excitedly, trying to peak up at him through her wing and hair. There was so much she wanted to tell him, she was feeling stronger now and hoped she wouldn't pass out again.

She raised her head and looked at him. Her heart started to race along to the rhythm of his own, her breath quickened at the sight of him looking at her again. She could see she had his full attention now, so she decided to tell him she couldn't speak to him. She pointed to her lips and shook her head no.

"You can't talk?" Darryl asked her curiously.

She shook her head no in answer.

That figured, he thought to himself. He looked heaven ward again and shook his own head at God.

Darryl lifted his hand to his hair and ran his fingers through it squeezing his overgrown black hair in his hand. He tried to think. Tried hard. When he looked back over at her, he dropped his hand and wondered about the sunlight. Why was she hiding?

She pointed to the sunlight and shook her head no again.

"Will it hurt you?" He asked remembering her hiss. That had to be it.

She showed him in his mind again, what he couldn't understand. The sunlight would burn her and start her on fire.

But why? He wondered, hating that anything could hurt her.

Darryl had to close his eyes then. He really didn't want to know. He tried to close his mind off the images he was remembering. He held her sweet, tender hand in his. He wouldn't let anything happen to her, but this was really going to be hard. Going out in the daylight was the only time he didn't have to worry about the demons. They couldn't go out in the daylight either.

Again, she showed him why. They, too, would burst into flames.

Darryl put his hands in front of him still holding her tiny hand, leaned his weary back against the wall behind him and bowed his head. The drug-like feeling he felt when she entered his mind was getting easier to handle now, but he still didn't like it.

Then it hit him. Like a wave toppling over him. When she had died so many years ago. He opened his eyes and looked straight down at her.

"It wasn't the SUV that had started on fire. It was you." She had taken on her angelic form to save his life, and lost hers for him.

Talia bent her head away from his. The pain was worse. But he understood now. She let the pain have its way and laid on him. She could die happy now. He knew the truth now.

All those years she had spent feeling guilty over her secrets she would no longer have to bare. For so long, she had spent wishing she could tell him the truth, now she wouldn't have to worry about it. By some miracle, he knew his destiny.

Darryl picked her up and pulled his angel all the way on top of him wrapping her arms and legs around him. She nestled into him and he let her. Holding her just felt right. Hugging her like he had always done felt better. He would keep her out of the sun; he would keep her safe here with him.

"I'll figure this all out." He promised them both.

He remembered what God had said to him. He had to go home. He didn't know why, but he knew he had to go. When the darkness turned into night, he would leave with her somehow.

She would be his. Hopefully she would be healed as well.

"Well, I guess this means I am your protector now." He said as he looked down and buried his face in her hair and wing.

Surprisingly, he felt her smiled back. She wasn't looking at him, but he felt it.

Darryl's heart almost stopped looking down at her so close to him. Her feathers, her robe, it was so unreal, but so surreal at the same time. She was breathtaking. Slow and easy, he leaned his head back up against the wall again and pulled her closer to him. His back was killing him now, but he didn't care about it because it only made him realize he wasn't dreaming.

He checked on her again at some point later after he ran through his mind all the different ideas and plans he could muster to get them home safely and he found that her wing had fallen away from around him. She was unconscious again.

Darryl knew what that felt like, and he let her sleep through it. It was better to be unconscious then to be racked with pain. He laid her down the best he could, and left her side only to take a moment to himself over by the windows.

Talia was listening into his thoughts but she was losing the fight with the pain she felt. It racked her heart and pained her mind. Her left wing was gone, and cut in places where it should be bending and stretching. She let the blessed unconsciousness over take her as he placed her gently on the floor and wished she could just disappear into the death that wasn't coming.

Things like this didn't happen to angels, she told herself as she drifted softly in and out of sleep. They didn't get torn apart. The touch of the demon should have killed her. Why was she still alive?

She contemplated, with a smile in her heart at her thoughts, why she was here with Darryl like this. As she drifted away again her mind filled with thoughts of a life with him again.

When she felt his arms wrapping around her body again lifting her back onto him, she hid the pain it caused her from him. She wanted to be close to him again.

Darryl parted some of her feathers and found her face. She wasn't looking at him, or so he thought she wasn't.

Talia kept her eyes closed even though she could hear his thoughts. She could feel what he seen when he looked at what was left of her wing. She wanted to touch it, hold it, and shield his eyes from it.

The desire to look at Darryl though, was so real; she couldn't not look at him anymore. He had saved her from the fight. He had fixed her up and stopped the bleeding. Her heart wanted to look at him one more time. So she made herself look up at him then.

Darryl was lost in thought about his men, as he stroked her face. He needed to get up and get out of here, but he couldn't figure out how. He looked down at her again and was surprised to see her black eyes opened looking at him.

Darryl breathed in a long gut wrenching breath. "Hey there."

He was still here, she thought. Still looking at me like that, she thought. Shyly, she turned her face away from him with a smile. She could feel the old stirrings of human emotions filling her like the strings of a harp being strung. It warmed her and eased the pain.

Darryl smiled just watching her. He rested his head against hers and let the silence pass between them. He needed to think. He needed the damn sun outside to hurry up and set.

Darryl thought about God then. He prayed to Him to move the sun for him. He prayed God would go before him and clear a path for him. To show him the way home.

Talia listened to his mind. Seen what he had seen. Darryl had found his peace with God. She smiled at her own thoughts. She would miss being God's angel. But she knew He understood the love between Darryl and her.

Darryl was remembering what God had told him. Home, he thought more about it. Was his family still alive? Had Asher kept his promise? Talia longed to tell him yes, but she needed to let him find these things out for himself.

Just as he was about to try and move her face up again and ask her if she was ready to go home, one of his men came barreling through the door next to them.

Talia reached for Darryl and clung to him, hiding herself under her wing.

Darryl addressed Johnny who had come through the door, as he tried to cover Talia with his body in his arms guarding her. "What is it?"

Johnny stood holding onto the door as he looked at Darryl and had to shield his eyes from the angel he was holding. It caused pain in Johnny's eyes when he looked at her.

"I found him!" Johnny shouted out the door. He looked at Darryl then and said to him, "We have to leave Darryl. It's morning. Bartley is hurt real bad. Patrick, Jimmy and I want to get the hell out of here."

Darryl looked back at Talia and needed to know what to do, but she was shaking and scared.

"What about the dogs?" Darryl asked, not really looking at Johnny. He had forgotten all about the dogs. Sentry had been gone for months now, but Cain and Judy were still alive. He hoped. He needed them to alert him to any dangers.

Cain peeked his head in the doorway then and looked for the sound of his commander's voice. When he found his commander, he walked over to Darryl slowly. He bowed down though in front of the angel his master was holding.

Darryl looked at Cain with relief and awe. Somehow Cain understood what he was going on. It made it that much more real for him.

"Cain, this is Talia." Darryl said as he introduced Cain to her.

When Cain looked up at him, Darryl smiled at him. Somehow, Cain understood this too.

Darryl felt Talia peeking out of her wing at Cain and it made him smile wider.

"Is she really... an angel?" Johnny asked aloud as the other men entered through the door behind him.

Darryl looked up at the men, his men. He didn't know what to tell them, but he tried.

"I don't expect any of you to believe me. I hardly know how to believe it myself." Darryl said as he looked down at his angel.

"Oh, come on man!" Bartley said to Darryl moving farther into the room, throwing his weapon over his shoulder. "Have you seen what we all have seen? Demons, vampires, zombies. We've seen it all. This..." Bartley had to stop himself short. "This is new, I'll give you that. But come on now."

"Who is she?" Bartley asked as he had to hold what was left of his bandage arm still so he wouldn't break open his wound again.

Darryl thought about his conversation he had with God earlier. "She's my angel. And she was struck down by one of those demons." He looked at Bartley then and tried his damndest not to cry. "It's Talia."

All the men had heard the story Darryl had told them of his past. Every single one of them took an awestruck step backwards.

Bartley chuckled aloud once he grasped the situation. "You lucky son of a bitch."

Darryl laughed too. Then he winced at the pain he caused her. Her eyes opened and so did her mouth, like she was crying out in pain.

"We need to get her out of here guys."

This came from Jimmy, who Darryl hadn't heard speak in days. Every one turned and looked at him also.

Darryl looked down at Talia when she settled down.

Talia peeked out from underneath of her wing she was covering herself with and shook her head no to him. She couldn't leave with him. He couldn't leave her either. She was afraid. She reached up her hand and placed it on his check and told him.

Darryl closed his eyes. He had never been so torn before. If he and his men didn't leave here now, the demons would return in the night and finish them off.

"What do I do Talia?" he whispered softly to her resting his forehead on hers.

Talia looked at him heart broken. She wished she knew.

"Take them all and leave, Bartley." Darryl told his second in command as he lifted his head. He knew his own future now, but theirs he was unsure of. "There is no reason for all of you to risk your life now because of me."

"But-"

"Just go damn it!" he told Barley. "Forget about the mission. There is no mission anymore." He told him looking straight at all of them. "You know damn well we have lost this war. It's over now. There isn't a government to protect anymore, or to protect us. This is all in God's hands now."

"You are all relieved of duty." He told them in an afterthought.

There was something bigger than all of them going on. New York was proof of that. He looked at Bartley and willed him to understand.

Bartley took a deep breath and walked over and knelt down next to Darryl. He couldn't look at the angel in his arms, but he could look at his friend. "With or without you, we have nowhere else to go Darryl." He didn't need to think about it anymore so he told Darryl, "I choose you." Bartley said as he sat up straighter to his commander. "You are my mission now."

Each one of his men knelt down too. They all bent their heads down also. It was a pledge of honor they all shared.

Darryl was awestruck by them.

Talia looked at the man Darryl was talking to.

She reached up to Darryl and touched his face getting his attention. She whispered to him: All wasn't lost. Everything he knew of in this world, his mission, his country, his duty; yes they were officially lost in this war between heaven and hell, but some things weren't. All that mattered now was survival.

Your men need you Darryl. I need you. We need them.

Darryl let her hand cradle his face. He took a deep breath of her essence. Her voice he hadn't heard in years whispered through his being like a melody.

He didn't know what he was supposed to do now. But he knew they would find their purpose together, all of them.

He laid his head back against hers. He smiled down into her hair. "You have me at a disadvantage dear."

Talia looked back up into his eyes confused.

"I thought I knew everything I needed to know to win this damn war. I was wrong. I needed you."

Talia grinned at him. If he only knew, she told herself. She lowered her head then. She curled her arms and nested into his body. She needed to rest in his arms. He was just going to have to wait for her to answer him. She didn't know what to do now or even say to him. She didn't have the power any more to find out either. God was just going to have to tell her... or not. She reminded herself.

Darryl explained to Bartley what had happened last night while Talia slept. He told him why they couldn't leave until the cover of night. Talia couldn't be in the sunlight. Jimmy and Johnny listened while Patrick stood guard.

Darryl held her and fell asleep along with his men and his dogs. He dreamed of the world around them. Fighting demons, protecting her.

Talia slept also. She had forgotten how good it felt to sleep. She didn't wake again till she felt the presence of evil in the building.

Looking around the room confused, she pushed her senses further for the source of evil she felt. She pushed on Darryl's shoulder and waited for him to wake. She listened to the evil crawling closer to them. She worried then and pushed harder.

When he finally woke, she showed him in his mind what was happening.

Night had fallen again.

Darryl stood then, lifting her in his arms. It hurt his back, but he had to. He needed to find a way out of the building and fast.

"Do they know you are still here?" he asked her as he lifted her up into his arms. When she nodded yes to him, he cussed aloud.

Darryl looked around them in the room. He kicked his men one by one and woke them up. His trained dogs kept silent but they stood at attention waiting for what they didn't know. He walked over to the door and peaked out. He had found the stairs he had been looking for last night, and turned to tell her where they could go hide.

Jimmy took Darryl's arm by surprise. He was holding his bluetooth in his ear and smiling. "It's Gavin."

Suddenly, they heard the sound of a fighter chopper flying above the building. Machine guns blazing, killing the demons that had swarmed the building.

Talia thought about standing to her bare feet while the men were talking, but her legs were weak. She hadn't walked on human legs in years. She could feel her weight in his arms and how his mind was clouded in pain from holding her.

Darryl was right there beside her to catch her when she tried and fell out of his arms. Her damaged wing kept trying to move and it hurt also making her shutter.

"I got you." Darryl told her in her ear. "You are still weak, don't try to walk." He told her as he smiled at her and held onto her.

Darryl nodded at his men and the plan they had formed. With his men in front of him, guns at the ready, they ran to stairs in front of them and headed for the roof.

Chapter Seven: Going Home

Darryl watched as the city below him faded away into the darkness of the night out his window in the back of an Army Special Forces Fighter helicopter. He was sitting in the back with Talia wrapped up in his arms, her wing was spread all around him. His heart soared with relief as the chopper rose higher knowing they were safe, so he kissed the top of her head while he watched his men hanging out both sides of the open doors in the helicopter. They would fight till their deaths to protect him and his angel.

He rested his head against the back wall of his seat and closed his eyes. He was safe for now up at this altitude. His men were safe too.

They had a two-hour ride back to the base in North Carolina, where Gavin had assured him, business was as usual even though all other communications were down. From there they would refuel and make the trip to Luna Pier. Home.

Darryl let his mind wander to the last time he had seen Talia alive out on the beach in Luna Pier. He had proposed to her, and she had said yes. He wondered now if that meant they were still engaged.

He looked at her then. Her head was resting on his chest and he wished her sleep sweet dreams. She was nestled in his right side, her left wing covered her entire body and wrapped around his left arm that was snuggled around her waist. Her lower wings covered his legs from the chill of the wind. Her head was buried under his chin.

He felt the movement of her hand that reached for his that was resting on her waist under her wing. She curled her tiny pale hand around his big rough hand and brought it to her lips and placed a simple kiss there on his palm that sent waves of rushing emotions through his entire body. She had done that many times in the past together with him. He hadn't even realized he had missed that gesture.

Darryl tipped up Talia's chin then. He looked in her eyes in the darkness of the night around them. He had no idea if he was allowed to kiss his angel. "Is it a sin if I kiss you? My angel." he intently questioned her.

All Talia could do in return was blush and shrug her shoulders. She left emptiness there in his mind that signified she didn't know. But she let images replay in his mind of all the times they had kissed in the past.

Darryl's heart raced in his chest as he took off his radio protection helmet. He looked down at the pale pink waiting lips of his angel and traced them with his thumb, and then he looked back into her eyes. He closed his as he found her lips with his own.

The touch of her lips on his felt warm and soft and she tasted like heaven. He held onto the kiss for as long as he could. He never wanted it to end. If he was going to die, this was going to be way he died.

He smiled when it ended and she questioned him why with a look. "It's nothing." He sighed greatly. "I was just expecting God to strike me down with lightening or something for kissing you."

Talia buried her head in his chest and laughed at him as she shamelessly read his mind.

Darryl couldn't stop himself anymore now that he knew he could so he tipped her head up again and kissed her more carelessly. He didn't hold back this time. He even sat her up in his lap and held her closer to him as he reached for her cheek and held her while he kissed her with all abandonment.

When he ended his kiss, he dragged his finger tip across her now red lips like he used to do. He watched as her lips kissed his finger tip and her eyes looked up at him. "I love you Talia. I still love you so much." he said to her as his lips quivered. "I almost can't believe this. I swear I'll never let you go." He whispered softly to her.

Talia hushed him with a gentle kiss of her own. When he rested his forehead against hers, she let his mind see a note she had written to him once before. It said "I love you a little more."

When she felt his smile in the darkness, she rested her face against his chest. She listened to his heart beat until she fell back into the sweet bliss of sleeping in his arms.

"Was it worth it?" Bartley asked him sometime later as he walked to the back of the chopper and sat next to Darryl.

"What?" Darryl asked him confused.

"Lighting strikes, death from God for kissing an angel?"

Darryl looked back and smiled proudly. "Yes." It was all he could say.

Bartley chuckled at that. They all had heard the transmissions over their radios of what Darryl had said to her even though he had taken off his helmet. And even though none of them could watch or witness it, they had all smiled for him.

"We should be landing at the base soon. Gavin says it is protected. Once we are refueled and ready, we can take off. Try to get her back home before sunrise."

Darryl nodded at that in agreement. He had no idea what to expect when they reached Luna Pier, he just knew his mission had changed and this is where he was meant to go.

Bartley then left them alone in the back of the chopper together.

Darryl watched as the lights of the base came into view. Gavin was right; the base was secure. Once they had landed, he left Talia alone in the back of the plane to talk with some of his commanders. He left Bartley in charge of her safety along with Cain who he ordered to stay.

Talia looked out her window and watched as Darryl talked with the men. She sighed gently and looked down at Cain and smiled. When Cain edged closer to her, she reached out and stroked his beard. She told his mind he was a good dog, and thanked him for all the years he had been by Darryl's side.

She watched as his little stub of a tail wagged in appreciation. He had always known she was there beside Darryl, but she had never touched him before, and he liked it.

Talia looked up and seen that Darryl was arguing with the men outside the chopper now and it worried Talia. When Darryl came back, he opened the door on the side of the plane and pointed at Talia. She watched as the man stood awestruck, confused by her presence. When he raised his arm up to shield his eyes, Talia curled up then on the seat and hid herself inside her wing.

Pain, unlike anything she had ever felt, raged like fire through her broken wing. It stung and pained her to move it. Darryl's healing powers had left her while he was distracted outside. The pain of it racked her.

Darryl climbed back in with his men who took up their positions again. He picked her up and sat back down with her in his arms. She could tell he still upset but she didn't question him on it.

Talia looked up at him and felt his own pain he was feeling. His back was hurt, but still he held her. She could feel the moment he felt her body, the moment he touched her, the moment his love returned full focus back on her. She loved him more for it. For the closeness he needed with her. For the love that over flowed out of him into her.

Darryl felt the small rise and fall of her breathing during the ride home. He looked up to the heavens outside his window and prayed silently. "Give me strength Lord. Give me faith." He looked down at her once more then. "Promise me that much also Lord."

He looked back up at the front of the plane then and noticed the man in the co-pilot's seat. It was Gavin.

Gavin had boarded the helicopter while they were parked at the base eager to be with the men on this new mission.

Gavin looked back at him then. He smiled an ugly smile and Darryl wished against everything that he wasn't with them on this mission.

Darryl heard Gavin's voice over the radio through his helmet and was glad Talia couldn't hear his cruel remark. Darryl leaned forward and replied to him. "You don't look at her. You don't think about her. Or I will push you out of this plane myself. Do you understand me?" He felt Talia's hand reach for his under her wing and held it reassuringly. He whispered to her not to worry as he stared down Gavin.

Bartley looked up then across the plane where Gavin was seated smirking at Darryl just a few feet in front of him. He took the liberty his commander couldn't. He reached forward and slugged Gavin in the face. Bartley then turned back to Darryl and smiled, and nodding at him with a wink.

Darryl nodded to his friend then. Gavin deserved so much more. He had every intention of doing bodily harm to him when he got the chance.

Taking a deep breath, he rested his head back against the back wall and looked back out the window. It took a long time before his heart slowed down and the anger seeped out of him.

The major at the base who was now in command of Darryl's mission hadn't believed a word he had said about an angel falling wounded to him until Darryl had showed him; he allowed Darryl to take the helicopter and his men on his new secret mission, with the understanding that he would report back to the base when it was all over.

Darryl agreed, but he knew there was no way he would go back and stay in the Army. He had served when most men had left and ran away. Cowards, they had all been cowards. Darryl knew he was no coward; he was just tired of living for a cause that was clearly lost now. His place now was at home with Talia and his family keeping them all safe.

Darryl closed his eyes and felt Talia's hand slip from his grasp. She creeped her hand softly up his chest and let it rest there. She shared in his mind with him moments in their past he had forgotten about. He watched as she filled his mind with music that made him feel lost in the moment with her, making him forget about everything else. No longer could he hear the roar of the wind in between the blades of the helicopter. He couldn't even hear his men talking any longer. All he could hear was her in his sleep.

"Darryl! Wake up man!"

Darryl was awakened out of his dreams to gun fire. He threw off his helmet and almost stood up.

"Talia wake up!" he tried shaking her arm, but she wouldn't even look up at him.

Blood. There was more fresh blood on her robe. He felt and looked all over her body for gunshot wounds. When he found them, he cussed out loud.

She had done it again, but this time it was bullets that she had taken for him. Her right hip and leg were covered in bullet holes and were bleeding. He reached up to her face and searched her head and chest for more wounds but found none. He reached inside his vest and drew out bandages. He ripped her robe apart from the hem up to her thigh and wound the bandages around her leg.

"Bartley, help me!" he cried.

Bartley looked over at him and climbed back in the helicopter. "We need to go man. What's wrong?"

"She's been hit! She won't wake up." Darryl pleaded.

"Bloody hell!" Bartley blurted out in his Irish accent as he inspected the body of the angel.

Bartley threw his gun over his shoulder and helped Darryl hold pressure on her hip while Darryl attached it down with medical tape.

Darryl tried to stand then and lifted her up, but his back started to give out. Bartley had to help him and lift him up out of his seat. He knew he had sat to long in one position and he cursed himself for being weak.

"You are not going to be able to carry her all the way there Darryl. We have a two-mile hike to Luna Pier." Bartley told Darryl as he shot another vampire who was getting close to them.

"Where the hell did they land us at?" Darryl questioned him befuddled, but as looked around the area where they had landed he realized they were on Whitby land.

Once they were safely out of the helicopter and ducked into the side of it for safety, Bartley pointed to the woods in the direction he wanted Darryl to go in. "Just keep going north Darryl. I'll find you. We got this." He told his commander as he showed Cain the way and told him to 'go see' ahead of Darryl.

Darryl looked back and watched the fight. Swift movements swirled around his men on the ground as the helicopter attempted to take off. He watched as they fired on the vampires and demons, but it wasn't long before the helicopter lost its fight with the demons in the air and crashed south of him in the open field. There was no way the pilots inside had survived the crash.

Darryl knew where he was as he tracked through the snow filled fields of the Whitby's land. He couldn't look back for men. He could only hope they would be able to follow him to safety.

He remembered as Cain lead the way through the woods, how Cain had felt around the Whitby's that night at Curtis' funeral. From what he had seen back in field, their land was littered with vampires. Somehow, she had been connected to them. They needed to get off their land as soon as possible. Cain had been right about her.

"Just a few more miles Talia. We are almost there."

Every so often, he had to stop and adjust her in his arms. She weighed more now that she was an angel, and his back was ready to give out from the weight of her. He had to stop once and fall to his knees; the pain was so bad. But the need to find Asher, to save her, filled him with the strength he needed to stand back up and run with Cain.

When he stopped again, Cain stopped and ran back to him, he licked his face and sat next to him keeping watch until Darryl could get back up and walk.

Darryl made it to the canal he remembered that crossed over into Luna Pier. Looking over it, he fell to his knees in disbelief into the snow that was falling around him now. There was a gate that was about 500 hundred feet in front of him on the canal and stood at least two stories tall. Just as tall as the wall that stretched on either side of the gate that probably ran the length of the canal.

He looked at Cain, then back toward the gate. He couldn't climb over it with Talia in his arms, but he couldn't push it open either. He lowered his head in defeat. There was no other way around it unless he took the lake, and this time of year the ice would be too dangerous to trust.

Darryl remembered his prayer then as he steadied his frantic heart and watched his breath billowing in front of him like smoke. He wasn't sure if it had come from Talia or heaven above, but he remembered it. "Give me faith Lord."

Before Darryl could finish his prayer, headlights blinded him. He had to shield his eyes and hold on tighter to Talia. Then he saw the unmistakable red and white flashing lights on top of the fire truck in front of him. He knew it was Asher even before he jumped off the truck.

Darryl looked at Cain just as his men, all of them he could see, picked him up onto his feet and helped him over to the gate where Asher was standing. Relief flooded through him.

It wasn't until Cain and Judy started barking and growling at the gate in front of them where Asher was now standing behind, that Darryl realized something was wrong. His men aimed their guns at Asher and asked for permission from Darryl to fire.

"No! Don't!" He hollered in command almost dropping Talia.

Bartley lowered his weapon and reached suddenly for Darryl, he steadied him, followed by the rest of his men. They were waiting for his next command, Darryl could see. Relief flooded him then.

He looked through the gates at Asher, his uncle, who was standing next to Curtis. Darryl squinted his eyes in disbelief then and looked at Curtis unbelievingly.

"Curtis?" he whispered aloud.

Asher walked closer to the gates so Darryl could see him in the moonlight. He knew why Darryl was here. Jordy had told him everything just moments ago.

Darryl could see the change in both men. He didn't have to look at Cain anymore to understand. They had been turned. For a brief moment, he doubted everything that happened to him. He had to have dreamt it all, he wondered.

It wasn't until Talia stirred in his arms for the first time since he had left the plane that he knew he hadn't been dreaming. She was still alive, and in his arms. She was still his. He looked at her then, and wondered what he was supposed to do now.

"It's not what you think Darryl." Asher told him raising his hands in surrender.

"You need our help. Let us help you." Curtis said to him standing next to Asher.

Darryl hesitated for a moment. It wasn't just his and Talia's life he had to protect. It was the lives of his men also.

Shelley stepped out from behind Curtis then. She walked up to the gates and looked for Darryl. "My name is Shelley. The angel in your arms is a friend of mine. Talia. Right?" She questioned him.

Darryl nodded his head toward her and looked back down at Talia. He wished she would wake up. He struggled with her again and lifted her higher.

Shelley put her hands up in surrender. She moved the gates open and walked toward Darryl slowly. She looked back for Asher and Curtis then. She asked them to follow her.

Bartley left Darryl's side then and grabbed Cain and Judy by the collars. They were still growling and didn't understand what was going on, but they listened to Bartley and stopped.

Darryl struggled again. His heart wanted to believe them. He needed them. But the woman in front of him he didn't know. He didn't want to trust her. He needed to plead with someone for help, whether it was his men or his family, or God who had sent him here, he didn't know. He just knew he needed help.

Darryl's heart started to race and his brow started to sweat. He was in pain struggling to hold himself up with Talia in his arms. He fell to his knees the closer the woman got but he held tight to Talia. He wasn't letting her go.

Shelley got down to her knees also on the snow in front of Darryl. She turned her head slightly and looked at Darryl. "You couldn't look at Him could you?" she whispered to him.

Confused Darryl asked what she was talking about.

"When you talked to God."

Darryl looked at her in disbelief. There was no way she could have known that. He looked back at Bartley then, who shrugged his shoulders not knowing what to say to him, then Darryl looked back at the woman. He nodded his head at then in acknowledgment to her question.

"He called you son when He talked with you didn't He? He sent you here to us." Shelley said as she looked down at Talia, then back up at Darryl sweetly. "Her name is Vestalia. I've known her since before you even existed. She is my friend and she knows me."

Darryl took a deep breath of relief then.

"I need you to follow us now so we can help you. God sent you to us for a reason. All you need to do is accept the gift of faith."

Darryl couldn't believe the words she was saying. Words Ken had spoken to him long ago he had forgotten, about accepting and faith, he remembered. There was no way she could have known that. It was the answer he needed. The answer to his prayers. He could feel the weight from the fear he felt lift off him.

Asher knelt down and looked at Darryl. "Your safe now man. I kept my promise." He added with a wink.

Darryl shook off the rest of the feelings and smiled looking down at Talia. Stunned, he noticed she was smiling up at him. He kissed her forehead and laughed aloud. "You could have said something you know sleepy head."

Talia reached up and touched his face. She told him there were just some things he was going to have to do on his own from here on out. But she would always be there with him when he had to do it. He would never be alone again.

Darryl looked at Bartley then who started to help him up. "These men, and this woman." He added looking at Shelley. "These are my family. They will not hurt us. Go with them." He instructed them.

Asher looked at Darryl and stopped him from moving while his men passed by. "Let me take her for you Darryl." Asher knew his back was broken. He knew what would need to be done. He offered what he could to Darryl. Asher would carry Darryl's angel for him. "I know what she means to you man. She is safe now. I promise. Let me help."

"But you can't touch her. She's an-"

"I know. I can now." Asher looked Darryl in the eyes and assured him nodding to him. He seen when Darryl noticed his eyes, and he knew then that Darryl knew exactly what he was now.

Darryl looked down at Talia in his arms. His broken, hurting angel. He wept then as he let her go into Asher's arms, it went against him to do it, but he let her go with Asher then as he wiped the tears off his face.

Bartley came up behind him then, with Johnny. They picked him up under his shoulders and carried his broken body to the fire truck.

At the fire hall, Darryl was laid on a table in the meeting room. All the pain of what had happened to his back filled his mind. The pain; he had been filled with adrenaline that had gotten him this far, that now left his body feeling every single ounce of pain he had fought through to forget about to get him here.

Darryl noticed the family of the woman Asher's girlfriend had been with was now standing in the room with him, his men, and his uncles. Frightened, Darryl also noticed they were all vampires. It was the first time he and his men had ever been in a room with vampires they weren't fighting with.

He looked up in the eyes of a man he didn't know. He could tell from his eyes and from Cain's reaction that this man was a vampire like the rest of them. He stilled Cain next to him and let the man talk to him.

"My name is Joseph, Darryl. Joseph Whitby." Joseph let that sink in for a moment before he finished. "Your back is badly broken. There is no way I can fix it here." Joseph sighed greatly then. "Even if we were in a hospital with the right surgeons they still wouldn't be able to fix what is broken Darryl."

Darryl closed his eyes then. He knew what that meant.

Joseph looked to Asher then. When Asher acknowledged his unspoken request, they knew what needed to be done. Jordy had already seen it and told them as much.

"There is a way I can fix you Darryl. I can make you like us." He told Darryl as he straightened up.

Darryl opened his eyes in a flash and looked at Joseph. He didn't understand, but yet, he did. And he didn't know how to react to it either. Everything inside of him was screaming in pain, and his mind was now screaming 'No!'. There was no way he could become one of them.

"We are not what we seem, Darryl. If you let me, I can show you everything you need to know about us. But then I will need you to surrender your life to me. It is the only way I can help you."

Darryl sighed unsteadily, then he looked around the room. He looked at Asher that was encouraging him now to listen to Joseph. He looked at Curtis, who had died, but was standing in front of him alive and well.

Talia. Darryl thought as he closed his eyes and then looked over at her. She was sitting next to him in a chair, holding his hand and willing him to believe. He squeezed her hand then. His broken angel, perfect and beautiful, was encouraging him also.

Talia smiled at him placing both hands now in his. She whispered to him, the only way she could while holding his hand. Faith Darryl. Have faith.

Darryl found the faith he had been looking for in her eyes. He always did. He looked back at Joseph then. "If I do this, will I still be able to be with her?"

Talia smiled and blushed at his question.

Joseph looked to Jordy. They both knew the answer to that question. He looked back towards Darryl. "Yes, as long as God allows it."

"Alright. Just make the pain stop."

Joseph and Asher shared a thought about Darryl's last thought. Darryl was about to experience pain far worse than this. But they kept that from him.

In a moment, what felt to Darryl like an eternity, Joseph showed him everything he needed to know, like Talia had done for him in his mind. Angels, demons, Earth from the beginning of time till now, God's plan for everyone.

Joseph showed him who they were and how they changed people. How he had changed Asher, and Curtis.

Then Joseph showed him Talia. How her life had been created for him. Everything she had ever done for him. Everything she had given up for him.

Hell! Darryl thought; she had given up heaven for him. Her love was unmistakably the best thing anyone had ever given him.

I love you a little more. She told him in a whisper through his mind.

When Joseph was done, Darryl turned and looked at her. "Thank you." He said to her. Not because he had to, but because he needed to.

And while he was looking at her he felt the worst pain he had ever felt in his entire life. Joseph was biting his neck.

Chapter Eight: New Life

Darryl woke up, face down in the snow-covered fields on the Whitby land. Darkness was all around him, but his vision was so pure when he opened his eyes that he could see the perfect snowflakes falling around him.

It felt like just moments before he had watched his men fight the demons they had been fighting alone, but now he could see beautiful sparkles in the snow that danced in the moon out here. There was no trace in the snow that anything had happened out here.

He sat up and could see far past the trees that led to the lake beyond and he could see the slushy waves in the dark that as they crashed against the ice that was built up close to shore; they pushed up grains of sand and pebbles; he could see with perfect clarity.

When he looked up into the sky, he could see the stars twinkling like never before, lighting up the darkness in the space above the Earth. He pushed his sight further and could have sworn he could see the edge of the firmament God himself had created for the heavens.

He turned at the sound of something unknown. What should have felt like his heart racing and his blood pounding through his veins, was a feeling unknown to him. It felt like fear racing through his body, but in the emptiness of his bodily reactions he was used too, he felt only pain.   It was just Joseph, he noticed, trying to calm the feelings he was unused too.

"What happened? What's happened to me?" He asked looking down at his hands that should have been shaking with fear. He felt... changed. He looked up at the man who had done this to him and questioned him. "Joseph?"

Joseph couldn't form the words of how he felt when he looked at Asher's nephew Darryl. He shook his head in the silence of the night at the awe he felt inside of the man. Darryl was the kind of man he had strived his entire life to be. There was goodness in him, a dutiful honor bound by a lifetime of giving himself to the purpose of protecting and serving others. In a way, Darryl was a lot like his sister, Emie.

"Do you remember all the things that I showed you?" Joseph asked him, standing in front of Darryl, still judging the man he had created, praying with fierceness that they had made the right decision in what they had done with Darryl.

"I do." Darryl could. "I remember... everything." He said astounded to Joseph.

Joseph smiled at that. He looked at the hard man he had created and looked heaven-ward, amazed. Some things just amazed him still. Like the newness of life he was watching right before his eyes.

"There are demons, Darryl, and then there are angels. We are angels, transformed. You are now one of us."

Darryl stood in amazement. He could feel his wings behind him spread out as he stood on their own accord. He stretched them, and flexed them, still astounded at the feel of their weight and height. His arms he flexed in front of him and looked over them. They were heavier than he remembered and the strength he felt within himself made him feel more powerful than he ever thought possible.

He was now like Talia, he thought to himself looking at his hands.

"Not exactly." Joseph told him slowly. "We are known as vampires, but not like the fallen ones you have encountered before. You are very different then her. That is why I brought you out here to explain it to you."

Darryl felt a rage building inside of him, but he held it still. He hated vampires. He had been fighting against them for too long to understand any difference. Joseph would have to hurry with his explanation.

"Very good." Joseph said to him as he felt the calm waging inside Darryl's storm. Joseph stood impressed. But he still eyed him with caution.

He started pacing around Darryl then. "First you will need to understand something. There are two things standing in your way right now. Me, a much stronger vampire then you. And then there is God who created you, and can destroy you if he so chooses. Do you understand?" He asked Darryl in a harsh, masterful tone. He almost pushed his will, but he was tempted to see Darryl make the decision on his own.

"Yes." Darryl said as he inhaled deeply and had to cough at the dryness he felt in his lungs. He tried to inhale again and the fire he felt there made him stop breathing all together.

Joseph stopped his pacing then. "A lot of your old habits like breathing will cease soon. You'll find that you will still do it out of habit, but you will learn it's not needed and more pleasing to abstain from it. Drinking will help with that, but we will cover that soon enough."

Joseph raised his hand, already anticipating Darryl's reaction when he figured out just what he needed to drink. "We will talk about that later. I promise. What you need to know is- what you really need to comprehend," he said to him in a more domineering voice, "is that God had a hand in your transformation. When I turned you, your body was burnt by Asher who has power over fire. Your body then was melted and infused with hot melting Steel of you and your men's armor." Joseph remembered then what they had done to Darryl, and he still couldn't believe it.

"I've never seen anything like it. Or would have believed it had I not witnessed it for myself." He watched the look that ran across Darryl's face as he looked down at his skin. It was one of disbelief also.

"Jordy and Shelley, they have the power to see God's future and his plans for us. They both saw what we needed to do for you. This is what they were told to do. What God wanted for you.

"You will no longer need armor to fight in this war. I assure you. Any vampire will be defenseless against you. There is nothing they can do to harm you or destroy you." Joseph almost chuckled as he thought that even he couldn't take Darryl down, but he coughed instead and left that thought to himself.

Darryl looked over and felt inside of his body. His skin was layered with a fine shine of steel. He shook his head and looked at Joseph. "How?"

"Like I said, you are a transformation. Unlike anything I have seen before. Vampire is what you are."

Darryl growled at him then hissed.

"Yes, there it is. That feeling you are experiencing right now, is why you are out here away from your friends and family at the fire hall. Away from Talia." He reminded him.

That last took Darryl back. He knew what vampires were. He had killed a lot of them. "How in the hell am I ever supposed to be around any of them again?" he shouted at Joseph. Every word he spoke grew louder until he almost let loose on Joseph.

Joseph looked at him with all his power. He took over Darryl's mind then. "You will listen to me. You learn everything I will teach you. And you will not disobey me. Then, and only then, can you attempt to go back to them. And if you still can't do it, then we will start over from the beginning.

"You will not hurt them. You will not turn to evil. Do you understand me?"

Darryl slowly looked away from Joseph, away from the doubt that was filling his mind and back up into the night above him. He wanted it so badly he could feel it inside of him. He had waited so long to be with Talia. He had thought he would never see her again. And now...

Well, now he could do this, he told himself. He would do this for her.

Determined he looked back at Joseph for help.

"You can." Joseph told him, reading his mind he took his attention again.

When Darryl really looked at Joseph though, hoping he was telling the truth, he could see inside his mind. He didn't know how he was doing it, but his mind could read the images there in Joseph's mind like he was looking at computer screen. He could flip through and sort out all the information he needed there in his mind.

Joseph responded to Darryl's thoughts with a nod of his head. I can see you also Darryl. He told Darryl cautiously. Joseph was still learning and never knew what to expect when he turned someone like Darryl, someone he didn't know, into a vampire like he was. He never knew which powers would be most prevalent in his creations. He could only hope God had a hand in it all.

Controlling his creations was just as hard as it was with his brothers. The newness of life, the newness of their powers, and the need to feed always controlled their actions.

Darryl would have to learn to listen, Joseph thought in his mind, showing Darryl his meaning.

Darryl eyed Joseph closely. There was much he wanted to know, much he wanted to learn. There was something in the power of being able to do what he was that made him eager and anxious. But his only desire, the only thing he wanted now more than anything else, was Talia.

"I've been where you are Darryl. I've seen others do it too. I have also seen others fail. You will not fail. I promise you Darryl. You have family and friends here. None of us will let you fail."

Darryl remembered everything he had shown him. "Your brother, Jordy. He's seen this right? He knew this was coming? He knows what will happen?"

Joseph looked away from Darryl then. Jordy knew what was going to happen. And God help them, he wanted to win. He wanted to save Emie. They had to. But what Jordy knew of Darryl, he couldn't share with him.

"He has." Joseph left it at that.

Talia opened her eyes. How long had she been sleeping, she wondered.

She looked around in the darkness of the attic around her through her wing she had wrapped around her parting her feathers and wondering what had happened that had awakened her. The only light in the dusty, ashy smelling attic was the light coming up through the stairs that led down into the fire house. She could barely make out seeing boxes of old fire gear and helmets. Dress uniforms were hanging from the rafters. Old, wound up fire hoses and odd looking decorations were stacked up neatly in boxes on the floor.

The smell inside of the attic was one she remembered all too well. It was the way the fire house had always smelled when she was younger growing up with Darryl. She smiled then at the memories of her younger self falling in love with not only Darryl, but also with his family. She loved coming down here then with Darryl to help his family wash the fire trucks. Every holiday the fire department always brought the trucks out to celebrate with the city and they always invited the children of the members, who looked forward to it, to come help wash the trucks up beforehand. Darryl would always bring her along to share in the parades or the family picnics the department would have for the family members on the department.

She woke then, worried about Darryl. She uncovered herself from her wing and sat up in the makeshift cot she had been sleeping on.

It hurt to move still, she thought as she reached for the wing that was no longer there. The bones in her back were healing slowly and were having a hard time not being able to move the damaged, broken arm of what used to be her wing. Every breath she took of air, every inhale along with the exhale, hurt as it moved her rib cage.

It had been days since she had seen him, she wondered thinking about Darryl. She knew Darryl was with Joseph now, and she prayed he was doing okay. She missed him so much, she thought to herself, trying not to move around to much as she hugged her arms around herself feeling for her broken wing arm.

The bandages were finally dry she noticed, she was no longer bleeding. She would have to thank Shelley for that, she reminded herself.

Talia heard a noise in the corner of the attic next to her that startled her. Slowly, very slowly, realizing that must have been what had woken her up, Talia turned her head at the sound of the rustle that she heard again. There, against the wall in the shadows, Talia noticed the figure of someone that spooked her. She quickly covered herself with her good wing, flinching at the pain it caused her, and tucked in her bare toes.

Talia waited and found herself peeking through her feathers at the figure and looked harder in the darkness. She noticed then it was just a little girl. The little girl was crouching down holding onto a little teddy bear that looked like a brown cat with a green plaid bow tie around its neck.

Talia wondered who it was in the room with her where no one else was supposed to be. Asher had promised her that much at least, that no one would disturb her up here.

Talia lowered her wing and looked closer at the little girl and was intrigued by her presence. Her long curly brown hair covered up much of her tiny body. Talia noticed as she looked harder at her that the little girl's eyes were brown.

Talia smiled at her invitingly, hoping the little girl would come out of the shadows. She had always had tenderness for children even though she had never got to spend much time with them.

"I saw you before a long time ago." The little girl spoke to Talia in the darkness of the corner, as she crept slowly towards Talia.

Talia nodded at her in answer. She wasn't sure if she remembered the little girl or not, but the little girl seemed to remember her, and that was ok with Talia.

The little girl was edging closer to Talia, and Talia noticed she looked frightened. When the little girl spoke, her voice was so sweet and tiny it tugged at Talia's heart.

"My name is Katie. You are my Aunt Talia; even though you are a... very beautiful angel, you are still my aunt, right? My daddy told me so."

Talia's heart melted then. This brave, sweet little girl was her niece. Ken's daughter. Talia had to cover her mouth as her own heart started to break. Her focus had always been on Darryl, and she had forgotten that after all this time she still had family too. Parents, a brother, and now a niece.

Talia wanted to speak to her then; she longed to tell the little girl in front of her how much she loved her. Talia thought she looked so much like Ken; it broke her heart.

Talia had found out that Ken had married Miranda right after high school while Darryl had been home visiting during Curtis' funeral. She was so proud of her brother and Miranda also. Looking at Katie now, Talia realized how much she missed over the years being so consumed with Darryl. She had missed out on her nieces' life.

"The night at my Uncle Curtis' funeral, you were sad, and holding onto Darryl's hand. But no one else could see you. Not even Darryl." This last Katie whispered to Talia as she climbed on the bed next to Talia and knelt there.

Talia smiled and nodded her head again. She turned toward Katie and lifted her leg on the bed so she was facing Katie. She couldn't believe this brave little girl was sitting here talking to her like this.

"What happened to your other wing?"

Talia looked over her shoulder and wondered how she could explain what had happened to her without scaring the little girl.

"S'ok. Uncle Asher said you couldn't speak. Is there something wrong with tongue?" Katie bent forward and tried to look inside Talia's mouth.

Talia had to hide her laugh; Katie was so sweet. She shook her head no at Katie then.

Katie looked down at her hands and twisted them in her Kitty's tail. Talia noticed the kitty's tail was worn out from Katie doing this so much, and she wondered if Katie did it when she was nervous.

Talia lifted her chin then and looked at Katie in question. She didn't want her to be nervous around her. When Katie looked at her, Talia could see the seriousness in her next question.

"Mommy said you weren't there that night at the funeral. But I remember you." She said defiantly.

Talia smirked at Katie. Children could be so misunderstood. She encouraged her to continue. Katie clearly had a question for Talia if she had braved her parent's wrath sneaking up here like this.

"Well, my Uncle Asher," she started hesitantly. "He is in love with an angel too, like you. She has wings too just like-" Katie looked at Talia's side that was missing a wing and looked back at Talia apologetically.

Talia almost shook her head in awe at this little girl. It was tender how she looked at Talia just then.

"She's an angel too, right?"

Talia nodded her head yes to Katie in agreement.

"Well, she's been missing for a long time. Do you know her? Her name is Emie." Katie asked excitedly.

Talia felt bad. She honestly didn't know her, but she had heard the stories of Emie and Asher. Talia was happy for Asher. Asher had never been the lady's man in high school, but all the ladies had wanted Asher, she remembered. Talia wished she could tell Katie she knew her uncle Asher. She hoped one day she would be able to share it all with Katie.

She shook her head no at Katie then in answer to her question.

"Well, Uncle Asher loves Emie so much. I think he loves her more than Mommy and Daddy love each. But no one loves anyone more than Mommy and Daddy love each other." She said smiling brightly at Talia.

"But Uncle Asher, he misses Emie. I find him thinking about her all the time." With that, Katie started playing with her kitty's tail again looking down at it. "I can tell he's thinking about her because he is so sad. Uncle Asher never used to get sad, he used to smile at me all the time, but now he is always sad and wants to be alone and he doesn't know I'm watching him." Katie said looking down at the floor beside her.

"He doesn't know I follow him sometimes…" She looked up at Talia expectantly then. "Will you help him find her? So he will smile at me again. I know he misses her, and I do too. But he's hurting, Aunt Talia and I miss his smile."

Talia felt the tears that weren't supposed to be there listening to little Katie's heart felt emotions.

Talia knew she was almost human again, she could feel it. She had to look away from little Katie then. When she regained her composure, she looked at Katie and nodded her head in answer to the little girl. In that moment, Talia would do anything for this brave, honest, sweet little girl sitting here with her.

She gently touched Katie's cheek and promised her she would help Asher.

Katie smiled brightly at Talia as she hopped off the bed and turned back to look at her. "I'm glad you are here Aunt Talia." Then she ran off as fast as her little feet could run out of the attic.

Determined, Talia got up then when she sure Katie was gone and out of sight. She gently stepped onto the floor beneath her holding onto the bed to steady her. Her legs were not used to walking yet, but Talia pushed herself.

She needed to go downstairs, she told herself, trying to hold herself up.

She wanted to see her brother Ken, she told herself while she took a weary step forward.

She wanted to see her old friend Shelley, and that meant she had to be able to walk.

Talia stumbled a few more times, and once she even let herself fall to the floor in pain. She hugged herself tightly then and thought of Darryl. She found the strength then to get up off her knees and walk. When Darryl returned, she wanted to be able to greet him, she told herself as she pushed herself around the room walking again.

Her good wing was making it hard for her as she walked around; it wasn't cooperating well with her. It wanted to lift her up when she needed to be down, and her broken wing arm kept trying to move with her other wing. It was frustrating, but eventually she got it.

Talia walked down the stairs from the attic into the bright meeting room. It took all her strength to be able to do it, but she prided herself in doing it. She hugged her arms around her waist seeing all the people that had gathered there. Everyone in the room looked at her in stunned silence and it frightened her. She knew they could see her. She knew they could see her broken wing. She could feel the pity they felt for her.

Talia had always felt shy and awkward around people. She was never one for grand entrances, or being in the spotlight. She always liked to fade into the background when she could. Unless she with Darryl. When she was with Darryl she felt like could do anything.

Now that she was in an angelic form, wrapped in the silkiness of a robe unknown to any human, she felt even more broken than before. She was different than those in the room with her. And she could hear what they were whispering in their minds.

She knew most of them though, she thought as she walked toward them in greeting. She tried to cover herself with her good wing, playing with her feathers in her fingers biting her lip, but the movement made her broken wing move too and she had to keep herself upright even though the pain buckled her knees.

Talia sighed as she looked away from the crowd of people in the room. She noticed out the little windows off the bar that it was night again. As she took another step she turned toward the bar and reached for it, but she missed and started to fall. Her wing tried to lift her but it was hindered by the floor under her. Her wings were much longer than her body. They were made for the air between these worlds; they weren't meant to be hindered by anything in their way, let alone her good wing was still learning to operate on its own without the other.

Her brother Ken walked up to her then and caught her in his arms hugging her, pulling her completely out of her thoughts.

"Hey, hey there. Hold on. I got you- Talia" He whispered to her.

When he looked at her all she could do was smile at him in greeting.

Talia hugged her brother tightly then. She had missed him so much.

"I know you can't talk, its ok, Asher told me." He told her gently, pulling her back to look at him. "Is there something you need? Are you sure you should be walking around?" He asked her looking at her bare feet.

Talia looked at him surprised. Katie had said the same thing to her about Asher. She loved that Asher had taken care of her so sweetly.

Talia raised her hand to Ken's chest slowly. She showed him an image of her friend Shelley. She hoped he would understand.

"You want to see Shelley?" he questioned her, shaking the drug feeling from his head.

Talia nodded her head at Ken and smiled.

"Just follow me. And go slow." He told his little sister as he put his arm around her and led her out of the meeting room and into the other truck bay where the fire engines were, where Shelley was.

"I missed you Talia." He said looking over at her while he helped her walk slowly.

Talia looked at him then and stopped him. She took his hand in hers and showed him in his mind that she had missed him too. A few steps later, she showed him how she had met little Katie. She showed him then how sweet Katie was and how much she loved her.

Ken grimaced at that. "We call her Katie Bear." Ken said laughing at himself. "She is hand full and is always in trouble. Whenever she doesn't get her way, she growls at us like a bear and stomps off. I'll hate to see what she is like when she's a teenager." He joked at Talia.

Talia laughed at that too. She could just picture Katie when she got older. Ken will have his hands full with the boys though, she thought to herself. Katie was beautiful. She looked just like Miranda too, Talia thought.

"I love them so much Talia. I am so grateful to Asher and the Whitby's. I don't know what would have happened to us had they not helped us all."

Talia was grateful too. She showed Ken as much as he led her to where Shelley was.

When they made it to the other truck bay, Talia noticed Shelley was talking to Curtis by one of the fire trucks. She could sense from Shelley the love she felt for Curtis and it made Talia happy. It was starting to look like everyone had fallen in love with someone while she was gone.

Shelley turned then to Talia's thoughts. She looked at Curtis and excused herself, as she left his side and walked over to Talia. "I got her Ken. Thank you." She told Talia's brother.

She smiled deeply at Talia. "What is it honey? What do you need?"

Talia looked at Shelley then. Her friend looked vibrant and happy. Her long spiral red hair was longer now then she had remembered it. She was so happy to finally see her again and speak with her.

Talia turned and looked at the radio room behind them. She needed to be alone with Shelley for some privacy so they could talk. She knew where everything in this fire hall was. She had spent most of her human life here with Darryl. She pointed toward the room and led Shelley to it. Shelley helped her walk slowly.

Shelley closed the door of the radio room and helped Talia into one of the squeaky chairs next to the long desk. She sat next to Talia and pulled her chair facing her. As she did, she looked down at Talia's bare feet and smiled. Talia had always been short, seeing her bare feet not being able to touch the floor under her made Shelley smile at the cuteness of the moment.

Shelley watched as Talia painfully adjust her wing into the sitting position around her. Talia sighed when she couldn't get it right and gave up all together when she reached for the other wing and realized it wasn't there anymore. Shelley tried not to smile at her, but she had missed her friend and it was good to see her again.

Talia spoke to her in a language only Shelley could understand. It was the old language. Her voice was high and piercing so she had to whisper for Shelley so no one else could hear.

Shelley understood her. She wasn't surprised at all that Talia was worried about Darryl. "He's ok honey. Honest. He's with Joseph. I've known Joseph for a long time. Darryl's in good hands." Shelley promised her.

"Joseph is teaching him how to adjust to his new life. He needs this time with Joseph."

Talia sighed deeply. It settled her feelings knowing he was doing well.

Talia then told Shelley about Asher and what Katie had asked of her.

Shelley smiled then at what little Katie had done and shook her head in amazement. Leave it to Katie Bear to be brave enough to talk to angels. "She's a feisty one that little one. It's been hard keeping an eye on her. You would think with everyone here it would be easy, but she is hard to handle." She told Talia honestly.

Shelley thought about what Katie had said then. About Asher and Emie.

"What she told you though, Talia, is true. Emie Whitby was captured and taken by her creator Victor. Asher is on a warpath trying to find her. He has spent time here trying to keep his family and this fire house safe, but she is all he thinks about."

Talia told Shelley that she needed to be with Darryl. How she didn't want him going alone without her. She all but begged and pleaded with Shelley.

"Oh honey, you can't."

She tried again when Talia started crying. "Honey listen. You are changing now, because he's not here with you. Your healing is slowing down. And by the time he has to leave, you still won't be strong enough to go with him. You are hurt just as bad as he was. You're not going to get better overnight honey."

Talia listened to her friend. She looked down at her own hands as Shelley spoke, but she didn't understand. She hated the demon who had done this to her, she thought looking away.

"You are going to be fine Talia, I swear it to you. Darryl will be safe with Asher. With all of us. I promise."

"Have faith." She added with a wink when Talia eyed her.

Talia laughed at that.

"I'll talk to Katie. She's a little mischievous, and throws fits when no one listens to her." Shelley looked more tenderly at Talia then. "Why don't you spend some time with her? You can meet Gabby too."

Talia looked at her in question then. Who was Gabby?

"Ken has two daughters Talia." Shelley told her knowing this was new to Talia.

Talia looked at Shelley in amazement. Gabby, she thought with a sigh. She was so proud of her brother in that moment.

Shelley smiled brightly at her. "You can help her keep an eye on Katie. The two of you need each other." Shelley thought aloud. The Kruse's were a stubborn bunch; that much she was sure of.

Talia understood then. She needed to listen to her friend. Shelley knew what she was doing, and she also knew what Talia needed to be doing. The last thing Talia wanted to do was be a bad example to little Katie. Talia was sure Katie wanted to tag along with her uncle Asher, and if Talia tried to go, so would Katie.

She had always loved children. She would love to spend time with the little girl who had so much faith. Talia wondered if she could learn a thing or two from Katie.

Shelley smiled at Talia's thought as she got to her feet. She looked down at Talia then. "Ken named her after you, you know."

Talia looked up at Shelley then in question.

"Her name is Katie 'Rose' Kruse. Just like your middle name."

Talia couldn't help the smile that broke out on her cheeks then. She was so filled with love for the little girl she had just met. She couldn't wait to see her again.

"Come on." Shelley told her, helping her to her feet again. "There's someone you should meet. Her name is Juliet."

Darryl had spent days without Talia when he had finally realized he had enough. "I've had enough Joseph." He said looking out on the darkness of the lake to Joseph who was behind him.

Joseph looked at Darryl curiously. He had known a few days ago that Darryl was ready to go back, he had just wanted to be sure.

Darryl, who was standing on thin ice out by the pier wall, turned and bared his fangs to his teacher. "A few days ago? What the hell Joseph!"

Joseph shrugged his shoulders playfully and turned to walk back along the pier back toward the fire hall. "Come on young student. Let's go."

Darryl jumped over the pier wall and followed Joseph back toward the fire hall. He tucked his hands in the pockets of his jeans nervously. "You really think I'm ready though, right?" He questioned him. He had a hard time in the beginning with things, but now that he was fed properly and Joseph had taught him how to obey his thirst, he had a pretty good handle on things. Or so he hoped.

Joseph turned and looked at him not stopping on their path. "Would I lie to you?" he asked him playfully.

Darryl thought about that. He could see Joseph wasn't lying. With all the abilities he could have developed, he was glad it was this one. He had the ability now to read people. He would need it to be with Talia. Darryl still wasn't sure if she would ever be able to speak to him again.

"She will. Your love is healing her Darryl."

"What does that mean? Exactly?" Darryl asked, not quite understanding what God had told him about that.

Joseph stopped in his tracks then and looked straight down Luna Pier Road without looking back at Darryl. They were almost to fire hall now. He wanted to make sure Darryl understood this before they got back.

"Love has a way of healing the heart and soul Darryl. Talia is not broken in body; her body is buried down the road in the cemetery. Her soul is what you see now when you look at her.

"She was ripped from the angelic life she knew, struck down by the demons who sought to kill you." He looked at Darryl then, with all seriousness in his words. "She had a mission like you did. To protect and save you. Now, that mission is obsolete, and has changed for her. She is unsure of who she is now, and will need your guidance and reassurance that she will be ok. That you will be ok. Once her soul heals, she will be healed. All Talia wants, like you, is to spend the rest of her existence with you, by your side. She only wants to love you. The best way to heal her now is to return that love she has given you, to her."

"Talia wasn't just born as a human Darryl. She was created as an angel in the beginning of time. When she took on the human form no one could see her as the angel she was here on Earth, not even you. When her human body died when she saved you, her soul went back to heaven. She came back then as the guardian angel by your side."

"When she was struck down by that demon, her soul should have died and went back to heaven. Another angel would have taken her place as your guardian. But God has other plans for her. God could heal her, but He is letting your love be all the healing she needs. The more you love her, the more time you spend with her, loving her, her wounds will be healed."

Darryl listened to every word Joseph said. It still amazed him, and frightened him. He still didn't feel he deserved her.

"God thinks otherwise Darryl." Joseph softly told him.

"I can't wait to see her Joseph. Show her those things. To love her. And tell her that now I can protect her. I mean, look at me!" He jested to Joseph triumphantly, proud of the way he looked, what he had become was everything Talia needed to be saved from all that sought to harm her. From everything that sought to destroy God's creations.

Joseph had to hide his next thoughts from him. There was a future he couldn't tell Darryl yet. That was between him and God. And he planned on being very far away from him when Darryl found out.

Joseph led Darryl back to fire hall where everyone was waiting.

Darryl walked through the doors of the fire hall a few moments later. He searched the crowd that greeted him, and thanked them all for their blessings. But it was Talia he looked for. He had to see her again.

Shelley walked up to him then, seeing his distress. "She's upstairs in the attic Darryl. She's resting. Go to her." She told him gently.

Darryl thanked her, and felt relief enter his being. He walked into Asher's room where the attic stairs were and walked up the steps into the attic. He found his way around the beams he had to duck under until he found the little room where Talia was sleeping.

The attic was old and smelled of fire and smoke. The men had used this attic for years, storing their old gear and equipment that was out of use. In the little room off the east side, was a cot and table that Asher had set up for Talia. It was quiet up here, and no one was around up here to bother her.

Darryl noticed as he watched Talia sleeping that she had her good wing wrapped around her body. Her sweet golden hair fell around her face and covered her wing. He stood there forever and felt the undeserving emotions he had felt years ago whenever he was in her presence.

He sat down on the bed next to her, and gently touched her arm. When she looked up at him, her eyes blinked a hundred times as she looked at him and he watched as realization hit her and she really looked at him.

Darryl. She whispered to his heart and mind as she covered up her mouth with her hand. She couldn't believe what he had become. He was like her now, but different.

Darryl looked down at his angel and touched her. He looked at her broken wing as she sat upright. He touched her feathers that were wrapped around her and let his fingers slide inside of them. He reached for her hand then and gently placed a kiss on her palm. Looking into her eyes, he told her "I love you Talia. All my life I have never loved anyone the way I love you."

He wiped the tears away that were falling down her cheeks and pulled her into his embrace. He sighed into her hair and smelled again the essence of her. "You are everything to me Talia. Everything that matters."

"God has given you to me now. He told me that my love will heal you." This he told Talia stroking her hair and looking deep into her eyes. "I want to make love to you, and just hold you so I can heal you."

She listened to and felt into his soul. The man she had loved her entire existence was holding onto her, feeling everything she had ever felt for him. His love was healing her now. She could feel it in every inch of her being.

I love you Darryl. She whispered to him reaching up for his face with her hands.

Darryl lifted her chin. He had to kiss her. Right now, he told himself.

When he kissed her, his whole body came to life. He held her cheek and kissed her deeply, lovingly, taking each of her lips into his slowly. With his lips, he promised her, and with his hands he held her, until she felt his love falling all throughout her angelic being.

He listened then to her mind and her soul. He followed her in the raptures he was creating in her. He touched her broken soul with his love and healed it.

Darryl lifted her then and pulled her into his lap where his hands crept up her thighs. He buried his face in her hair for a moment and just smelled the sweet aroma that was her. Then he started pulling off his borrowed shirt from the fire department and returned his lips to hers. He sucked her lips into his and held them there inside his mouth. His hands found their way into her hair and held her down against him until he could feel her melting in his lap. And then he did it again, cradling her.

Talia felt everything he was doing to her like she had once felt long ago. But now, now they were something different then the young humans they had been. Their flesh wasn't made of weak skin. Their flesh was strong, thick, and powerful. It was rich with nerve endings that made them feel more than any human ever could. Their passion wasn't sinful temptation, but fueled and flamed with love. They were stitched together and blessed by something greater than this world could ever imagine.

Darryl stopped kissing her as his fingers drug down her back. He felt the silkiness of her robe on his fingers and her back beneath it. Her eyes were closed as she felt everything he was doing to her body. He stopped at her bottom and found her thighs again where he crept up her robe to her skin beneath it with his hands. He pulled her robe all the way off her body and kept his eyes on her eyes watching as she smiled at what he had done.

Talia reached into his hair with her hands. She let her fingers tickle the back of his neck while she parted his hair with her fingers. She made him look up at her and placed a sensual kiss on his lips.

Darryl found his way down to her thighs with his hands then he ran them back up to her bottom. He watched as she threw her head back in a moan and he kissed and sucked on her neck as he let his hands roam on her bottom. He pulled her closer still squeezing her bottom in his hard hands till he could feel the warmth of her woman hood on him.

Talia fell under Darryl as he laid her down. He stood briefly to remove his pants, only to fall back down on top of her again. He propped his body on top of hers so not to crush her back and damaged wing. He smiled in his kiss knowing exactly how she felt. He kept their bodies together and moved up further into her by lifting her leg at her knee with his own. He relished in her moans she was making. He kissed down her neck and fanned the flames she was experiencing. With every touch of his lips on her he kissed her tenderly and sweetly. He whispered his love for her across her chest as he made love to her breast he adored.

Only once in the back of his mind did he remember what it felt like to live without her. He promised her heart, her mind, her soul; that they would never have to feel that again.

Darryl kissed her lips again. He heaved his thumb across her lips and then he trailed his kiss down her body again. He explored her and stirred a passion so great in her that he could hear her beckoning to him inside of his heart and they both wanted more.

His hands never left her body. His eyes never closed.

Darryl took his time making love to Talia. He stayed with her for days, dreaming and laughing with her. They shared more than just moments in the days that past. They shared a lifetime.

Darryl played with her hair and feathers that were lying around him. Talia had fallen asleep on him some time ago. He hadn't wanted to disturb her, so he had just let her sleep. It was the knock on the attic door that woke her.

"Shh. It's just Asher." He told her as he touched the worried look on her face.

Talia looked up into his eyes. She knew he had to go. She knew where he was going. Tears she couldn't stop fell down her cheeks. She told him how she didn't want him to go.

Darryl kissed her tears away and pulled her closer. "I swear to you, I will come back to you. There is nothing in this world that can stop me."

He looked into her eyes that were black and void less. His love was healing her. But her heart was hurting now. She was running her fingers across his chest worried. He could see it there.

He tipped her chin up and made her look at him. "Have faith." He winked at her.

Talia grinned at that. Of all the beings who should be able to have faith, it should be her. She just knew God had a plan, and she didn't know what that plan was now.

She looked at him though, knowing he needed to know she was going to be okay. He needed her strength to get him through this. She whispered to him then. She told him she would ok.

"That's my girl." He said reading her thoughts, stroking her hair that had fallen in front of her. "I could use a kiss goodbye too." He grinned at her.

Talia took a breath as she leaned forward and kissed him. She kissed him long and hard and held tight to his arm. She didn't want to let him go.

Darryl walked downstairs with Talia and greeted every one downstairs sometime later. The stronger she became, the easier it was for them to be in the same room with her without feeling pain as they looked at her. Darryl even noticed she had developed a giggle.

He noticed from beside him, she was looking at him, at his thoughts, with a smile. He had to let go of her hand as little Katie made her leave his side to show her something, and he was fine with that. He watched as Talia looked back at him with excitement on her face. She had always loved children growing up. The fire house was full of children for her to satisfy that need with.

Talia was safe here, he thought, like everyone else here and it seemed they all were taking to Talia the way he had. They were all very happy to see her.

Darryl heard the unmistakable gasp of his mother from behind him. He turned a little too swiftly around to see her. He watched as his wings blew right through her body that she could not see, and watched as the rush of wind caused her hair to move out of place a little.

"Oh honey…" she gasped again, this time covering her mouth. She couldn't believe what she was seeing or contain it.

His father and mother had been sleeping the night he had returned with Joseph and they had not seen him yet. He looked at them now, and seen in their eyes what he looked like to them. As impressed as he was with Joseph and Asher's work, it was the proud feeling his parents felt for him that made him feel loved from the top of his head to the boots on his feet. He was the picture of safety for all of them now. More than he had ever been before.

All he could do for his mother now was open his arms and wrap her in his solid embrace and close his eyes at the cherished thoughts his mother felt for him now.

When she stepped back to look at him again, Darryl looked at his father behind her. "Well dad?" he questioned his father as he took his hand in his and shook it like a man. "What do you think?" He asked, standing back grinning at him.

His father looked at him. "You look like a superman son." His father laughed.

"Oh no! That's my title." Asher said to Darryl as he walked in the meeting room with them.

"Well, you know how it is Asher." Darryl told him grinning from ear-to-ear. "Someone always writes a better squeal than the first. One where the new superhero makes all the ladies weak in the knees." He told Asher with a wink.

"Keep that up kid, and I'll paint that steel body of yours red and green and call you Joseph's sidekick." He said grinning back at Darryl.

Darryl had to think about that one and caught on to the superhero joke he had heard about Joseph being Batman. He laughed, knowing there was no way he was anyone's side kick.

"We have a saying in the Army Asher. What doesn't kill you only makes you stronger. And I feel a hell of a lot stronger than I did a few days ago."

Asher smiled wide. He bumped fists with Darryl. "We each got something to be proud of kid. I am so proud of you."

Darryl knew that feeling too. It was written all over his parents' face that were now looking at their heroes all standing in one room together. Joseph and his brothers were standing by the kitchen; discussing the meeting Asher had called Darryl to. Curtis and Shelley were now talking to Asher. Darryl could see what they were feeling now and was glad he was a part of this.

For the last few months of 2015, they had lost hope. Now that it was 2016, looking at the men who had stepped up to save the world and the lives of everyone here at the Luna Pier Fire House, he felt safe. Safer than he had in years.

Darryl watched as his men walked in the room and took in the sight of his new body. He could read it in their minds how they felt about him now. Their pride in their commander was still there in their hearts. They were ready to fight along beside him just like they had done before.

Darryl walked up to them and shook the hand of Bartley. "Hey, thanks man."

"For what?" Bartley questioned Darryl looking back at him. Darryl didn't let go of his hand then. "For getting me here. It means a lot to me that you had my back man. Literally." Darryl told him in a smile.

"That's what we do." Bartley told him, nodding and bumping fists with Darryl.

Darryl then looked at Jimmy, Pat and Johnny.

"We will follow you anywhere." Johnny told him proudly.

Joseph walked up to them then. "We need to talk to your men, Darryl."

"Yeah, sure." Darryl said to him, as he led the way for his men to follow him. They sat down at the tables in the meeting room.

Joseph looked at everyone who was in the room now. He asked Darryl's parents if they minded stepping out of the room. He had a meeting to get started now that Darryl was ready.

Once everyone was out of the room that didn't need to be in there and the Whitby's were all seated at the tables, Joseph stood in their midst. Darryl's men, who were still congratulating Darryl, were seated with them too. He needed every one of them to help in fighting this war, but first they needed to get the new fire house finished for the safety of the ones left behind.

Joseph addressed everyone at the tables. Asher had lined the tables together in a horse shoe shape so everyone would be facing him. As Jordy came up and stood next him, Joseph smiled at the shirt he was wearing.

Asher had one of the girls who worked in town make new t-shirts for everyone in the fire house. Joseph realized he was the only one not wearing one in the room. He looked at Asher questioningly, and caught the one he threw at him from behind the bar.

Joseph smiled down at. It was a blue t-shirt with a white Maltese cross patch on the left side. It read 'Luna Pier Fire House' in bold white letters around the outer edge of the cross. Behind the cross, instead of the white flames that had been there before, there were white angelic wings behind it. He never would have guessed he would be wearing one before all this. But now that he was a part of this family, he knew he'd wear it with pride.

Joseph took a deep breath and looked over at the tables at everyone. It was time to get everyone on the same page.

He smiled brightly at them, and started the meeting. "I just wanted to thank each of you. We have kept this city together and its citizens safe. It has been hard, but without each of you, we never could have pulled this off.

"With the addition of Darryl and his men, I think we can finally get this house finished. It's starting to get a little crowded now, but everyone is working together and doing their share around here.

"The buildings next door; the old bar on our left, and the little strip mall came down nicely yesterday. We owe Jimmy a huge thank you for getting those cameras installed outside." He said nodding to Jimmy who stood up and took a bow at the hoots and hollers from the crowd. "It will be much easier now working outside at night with those cameras around town. And keeping an eye on the humans when they are outside." He added in an afterthought. They had lost a few of them, and Joseph was determined not to lose anyone else.

"If we work around the clock for a few more days, we should be able to finish this project so we can move onto New York. Darryl we need to talk to you and your men about that."

Darryl's mouth felt dry at the mention of New York. He was ready to return, he was ready to fight. But he was not ready to leave Talia yet. "Just tell us what you need."

His men all gave their agreement next to him, Joseph could see.

"A bigger plane." Shelley stated plainly from next to Curtis.

Darryl looked at her questioningly and then looked back to Joseph.

Joseph made a face to Shelley in disapproval. She was jumping ahead of him. "My sister, Emie, as I'm sure you have all learned, was kidnapped back in June when this mess started." Joseph walked over to the bar to retrieve pictures Jordy had taken while they were in New York. He handed the stack to Darryl.

"These two men-"

"Victor and Axel." Darryl said, sighing as he looked at the pictures and passed them to his men.

Joseph placed his hands on the table in front of Darryl. "You know these men?"

Darryl looked Joseph in the eyes as he sat back in his chair. "Yes." He said sliding his hands in his pocket. "We were sent to New York last year after the fall of the White house in August. There was word, that the trade center, is owned by this man," he said pointing to the pictures. "Victor and his enterprise of vamps are the ones responsible for the attacks here on the US. It was our mission to find them, study them, and kill them."

Joseph took a deep breath as he turned and looked at Jordy who nodded in agreement with Darryl's words. Good, he thought. "So, you know where they are now?"

"Jimmy, hook up the tablet to that television, will you?" He said to Jimmy who was next to him.

Jimmy shot up, pulling his tablet out of his bag and walked behind the bar to the system where he could set up their mission tablet to be displayed on the television.

Asher stood up then. He walked over to the pictures Darryl had laid out in front of him. "What about this man?"

Darryl looked at the picture in front of him. He did a double take back at Asher. "His name is Axel…" Axel looked just like Asher, Darryl thought to himself. He hadn't noticed it before.

Asher stood up tall. He took a deep breath before he addressed Darryl again. "It is a long story Darryl: one I will tell you later. These men," he started to say as he pointed at the pictures. "They have Emie. And I will be the one that kills them. Very slowly. But first, we have to save Emie."

Darryl looked at Asher. He understood what that meant. "I'll be right there beside you when you do. Uncle." He smirked at Asher to lighten his mood.

Darryl stood up then and walked over to the TV. Jimmy handed him the tablet, then he took his seat. Darryl flipped through the folders of their top-secret mission that no longer existed. He showed them the pictures they had on file of the city and the surrounding area. He showed them pictures of the trade center they had taken, and opened the files he had on the tablet of the floor plans they had of the building. He also showed them and described to them details of Victor's men.

Darryl showed them all the gruesome footage they had from the attack on Antarctica. He watched as the Whitby's and Asher leaned forward and took in everything that had happened. None of them had expected to see the demons. It was new information to them.

"When they attacked us at the house, just before you and your men arrived, we noticed some of them then had the ability to strike at us like that." Joseph said as he stepped closer to the TV and showed Darryl in the footage what he meant. He stood there awed by their power. "If it wasn't for Asher, we never would have made it out of there. The way their claws can slash like that." He showed him in one scene. "They could slice right through us and kill us."

Darryl noted that and continued. "We've only seen them on remote islands. And only before the attacks on the US. It wasn't until all communications went down that they appeared here. We think Victor was waiting for our military to stop fighting before he called them here. Once we landed in New York, it was like they had been waiting for us. They knew everywhere we were and attacked us hard."

"If you don't mind us asking, how many of your special operation teams are there like yours?" Jordy asked Darryl.

Darryl looked down at his tablet then. He shut it off then and looked back at Jordy. "There were three teams like ours. We trained in Ireland with the UN. There was a British forces team, and two Army Intel teams."

"Where are they now?" Joseph asked.

"We lost the British team in a raid on the streets in London early last year. Bartley and Johnny are all that's left from that team. And then our other team was lost protecting the White house. My team is the only surviving special ops team left in the world to fight against this.

"One of my commanders who is the head of Intel down at Fort Bragg right now is putting together another team, but they are busy down there trying to protect what's left of the base, and what's left of the government. I don't see them being of any use to us."

Asher was leaning against one of the tables facing Darryl instead of sitting down. "We have a better plan Darryl. Better than going in guns blazing." He nodded at Jordy then.

Jordy smiled at Darryl then. "What do you remember of 9/11?"

Darryl remembered it very well. He had been in high school then. 9/11 was one of the reasons he couldn't wait to graduate so he could join the Army. "I learned that Victor was behind it all. We think that is how he was able to acquire ownership of the building."

Darryl watched as Joseph, Jordy and Jeremy; who was sitting next to Shelley, Curtis, and Asher, all looked at each other and cussed silently.

"We think Victors plan then was to shut down our economy, then shut down our communications. The fall would not only damage our emergency personnel as they gathered together and worked down at ground zero from all over the country in the timing of it all, but he also tried to destroy our military that day. That's why he hit the pentagon. He used humans in the attack who failed miserably on his planned targets. What most of the world didn't know was that the military intercepted a lot more planes that day with a lot more planned targets.

"He wasn't ready for our strength or the fight that we gave him.

"What we haven't learned yet, was why. Why he chose New York. Why he is still there now."

Jeremy spoke up then. "It's all Asher's fault."

"Hey!" This, from Asher, who didn't like Jeremy's comment.

"No, seriously. It is." Joseph looked at Darryl then with all seriousness. He hated talking about Emie, because it only made him miss her more. And he really hated knowing this all was Asher's fault, but Asher was starting to grow on him now a little. Joseph also knew if anyone was going to bring his little sister safely back home, it was Asher.

"Yes, Victor wanted the trade centers that day. But Asher was in New York that day. The severity of all, the greatness of the destruction on the city, was Victor trying to destroy Asher. And yes, he failed miserably." Joseph told them all as he watched Asher try to decide whether he should be proud of himself for surviving it all.

"Victor comes from a royal bloodline of vampires that goes back to the dark ages in Europe. They have been planning the destruction of humans for centuries. It is us, as the protectors on this Earth, who have always averted their attempts.

"In this new day in age, it is harder for us to be everywhere all at once. The world population has grown, and along with it so has the evil in this world. It was easier for Victor and his family to plan this out than it had been in years past.

"It was easy for him also to recruit the help of other nations. I'm sure the destruction of the US is on many people's hit list." Joseph said this last to Darryl who agreed.

"We, meaning my brothers and my sister, were born in England in the late 1800's. Victor, in all his devious planning, found Emie one night outside alone. He learned, by some ability he has to see in humans what their power is, seen that Emie would have the ability to control the minds of humans. She can make them see whatever she wants them to. She can even make herself invisible to them and walk amongst them. And she can make them feel emotional whatever she wants. It is a powerful ability. In the wrong hands, it could be used as a weapon.

"Victor knew this. Another ability of his is that he is seer. He can see and visualize the future.

When he found Emie, he took her life and turned her. But my father came outside that night with a torch and stopped Victor before he could kidnap her. He lost Emie after that night. My father made Emie leave because she was a vampire. He was afraid for all of us. Emie left us for over a year. None of knew where she was. Victor has been hunting her ever since.

"When Emie came back to us, she found our mother had passed away from an illness she had spread to our family. Our father died shortly after." Joseph looked down at the ground then. He knew the sacrifice Emie had made then for them. He couldn't imagine now if she hadn't. "Emie, she didn't want to be alone anymore." He said aloud, struggling to be able to finish.

"Faced with losing her brothers who loved her, the only family she had left, she made the decision to turn us. She knew the good she had found within herself. She hadn't turned to evil like most vampires do. She made sure we didn't either. She took my life first as we experimented with it. Then she took Jordy and Jeremy." Joseph looked over at his brothers then. They were both sitting next to each other. They had both become everything Emie wished they would become.

"We learned her ways. We learned not to kill the humans who God had chosen and had a plan for. We only took the lives of the ones He wanted and required. Because we didn't turn to evil, because we choose to live this life, God has blessed us.

"He has called on us now. We are to fight in His army, alongside him, to defeat the enemy and destroy the evil." Joseph found the welling of his emotions ran deep. He said each word with meaning.

He looked directly at Darryl and his men. "Will you and your men stand with us, help us find my sister and bring her home safe, and then destroy this evil that has taken over this land and send them back to hell?"

Darryl's men stood with no word from him and they started to chant. Their military creed that resonated in their hearts at Joseph's words and emotions. They stood still, tall, and proud sure of every heartbeat that resonated in their hearts.

Darryl smiled at them, then to Joseph. "I think that's their way of saying yes."

Chapter Nine: Asher's Plan

Asher stood outside the fire house the night before he and his family would depart for Fort Bragg. He looked at the house they had built. With the help of Darryl's men, they had created a steel fortress that was incredible, and it was indestructible by any enemy.

And it was a home. For not only his family, but also for the people of this city that were left that he would be leaving behind, it truly was a home.

Joseph, and his baby sister Izzy would be staying here to protect the city and this house while he was out saving the world and bringing Emie safely back home.

He looked at the sign he and Ken had hung over the bay doors where the trucks were parked behind. It read bold and proud 'Luna Pier Fire House'.

Darryl came out the front doors and stood next to Asher in the road then. He looked back at their creation. It was everything Asher thought it was.

"So this plan?" Darryl asked as he lit up a smoke next to him.

Asher looked over at Darryl with a grin. "It's a grand plan."

Darryl laughed out loud at that. "I bet it is."

Asher looked back at the firehouse. "It's a little ironic, but Shelley and I both agree that flying a plane into the tower is the best way for us to get in the building."

"Because walking in the front doors would be too easy?" Darryl jokingly questioned Asher.

Asher looked over at Darryl sideways at his joke.

"I'm just playing man." Darryl said to him putting his hands up in surrender.

"As I was saying, since the city is full of Victor's minions, we need to be able to make a surprise attack on Victor. Using his plans to destroy the city the first will be the same way we do it. He will never expect it." Asher told him, hoping his plan was as solid as it felt.

"Just one thing I don't understand. How do you plan on surviving the crash?" Darryl asked him honestly. He knew crashing the plane into the tower would cause an explosion none of them could survive.

"That's where Curtis comes in to play."

Darryl smirked at that. This plan of Asher's was starting to sound more and more like the high school football plans they used to strategize together.

"Curtis can transport us with him when he disappears. Shelley can put the plane in autopilot and Curtis can transport us all to the ground safely. Then he can transport me and Jordy to the floor where they are holding Emie.

"Cristina has already seen the room where Victor is hiding Emie. She has shown it to Curtis, and he is pretty sure he can put us on the right floor, or close to it. Jordy can figure out the rest once he's in the building."

Darryl saw the plan in Asher's mind. It truly, just might work. "Definitely a grand plan. But, where do you plan on getting a plane of that size that can do that much damage?"

Asher looked at Darryl then. "That's where you and your men come into play."

Darryl looked at his uncle unsure then. He eyed him curiously.

"You are going to get us down to Fort Bragg. We will need a plane bigger than Shelley's passenger plane and bigger than a commercial plane."

Darryl knew that on the base in Fort Bragg they had many military planes. Including a transporter plane. "Will a C-130 work?

Asher nodded his head at Darryl then.

Darryl could picture it then. A plane of that size could definitely make this plan work out nicely. Then a thought entered his mind. "How do you plan on getting all of us down to Fort Bragg Asher?" He questioned Asher.

This one question should have foiled Asher's plans and Darryl hated asking it, but it had to be asked. The path there would surely be filled with demons and vampires that would be attacking them at every turn. Not only that, but the snow-covered roads and ice in the dead of winter would surely make driving there in any vehicle dangerous. It would be dangerous for not only Darryl's men, but also for the Whitby's who would have to fight against this enemy also.

Asher smiled then. "My fire trucks."

Darryl looked at him questioningly handing him a smoke that Asher lit for him.

Asher smiled, still looking at the house, as he lit his own smoke. He let Darryl see his plan, and how it had worked before. The men could hide inside the steel tank of the fire truck to protect them.

"They won't hide, they will fight."

Asher shrugged his shoulders. "That's up to them. But that's the plan."

Darryl thought about the fire trucks. Of all the vehicles that could make it through the snow-covered, icy roads in the winter time, it was a fire truck.

Darryl tucked his hands in the pockets of his jeans and sighed. He had a few more questions for Asher now that he had his attention. "How come you never talked to me about Emie when I was home on leave?" He hesitantly questioned Asher.

Asher took a deep breath of the fresh, ice cold air in the night. "Because I knew what she was, and I had no clue how to tell you.

"The night of Curtis' funeral was the night I learned Emie and her family were vampires."

Darryl thought back to that night. Asher had been a mess, but Darryl had never guessed that was the night Asher had learned that little bit of information. It must have been hard for him, Darryl thought to himself.

Asher shook his head at the memories. "Her brothers, being brothers and doing what brothers do when they are trying to protect their sister, decided to scare the hell out of me in their home that night. I saw something different about them though. They weren't just men. I kept feeling this weird feeling, I can't quiet describe it other than like I felt like I was being hunted, but it over took me. And in one second, I was sitting there smoking with them, and next I said aloud to myself 'Vampire' thinking that's what the boys looked like, and then it was there, in their eyes, their fangs. I saw who they were, and boy did it scare the hell out of me!" Asher chuckled aloud.

Darryl wanted to laugh with him, but he knew the scared feeling Asher had that night. He had it many times before in the past fighting against the demons.

"Emie was up in her rooms preparing herself for the funeral and didn't know what her brothers had done. They had left, of course, before she came down stairs, knowing exactly what they had done to me and her.

"And Emie tried that night to talk to me, but I was so caught up in my own selfishness that I didn't even stop to take a moment and talk to her."

Asher thought about all the horrible things he had thought about in his mind that night. All the things Emie could read in his mind that weren't really how he felt, they were just poor reactions.

Darryl listened into Asher's thoughts then, trying to understand what Asher was thinking. He learned how Asher regretted not talking to Darryl, and how Asher spent the next year without Emie.

He also learned everything he wanted to know about Emie. The way Asher thought about her, the way he loved her; Darryl knew the woman he was about to go and save was worth it. Emie was just about as wonderful as Talia was.

Asher's anger started to heat and build up inside of him. Darryl could not only feel it, he could see it in the way Asher, who wasn't smoking a cigarette anymore, was blowing out smoke through his nose.

Darryl could read in Asher's mind what he was thinking about. For the first time, Darryl seen what Victor and Axel had done when they had kidnapped Emie. Asher had selflessly given his life for Emie that day. Asher hated that Victor had Emie now, and that Emie was living all this time thinking Asher was dead. She had no idea that he was still alive.

"Care to fill me in on your twin?"

Asher looked at Darryl then. "I'm going to kill him."

Darryl looked at him too. "Yeah. I know." He waited for Asher to answer him then.

"My parents didn't know they were having twins till we were born." Asher said quietly staring back at the firehouse. "They never told anyone other than close family, and after his death, no one spoke of him again.

"Just a few days after we were born, my parents were down in Point Place by Toledo; they were visiting family and sharing the good news." Asher told him, lighting another smoke and tucking one his hands in his pockets. "On their way home, it started to snow and my father slid on the ice on the road and hit Joseph's oncoming car. He was sent off over the edge of the road into the water in the canals on Summit Street. The ice was thin on the water and his car started to sink in the icy waters. Joseph was able to save my mother and me, but he didn't go back in for my brother. He thought he was already lost."

Asher put his head down at the feelings welling inside of him.

"Victor was out there that night. He must have been following me, or Joseph, we are not sure. But he pulled Axel from the wreck. He saved his life and kidnapped him that night. I don't know all the details of how he raised him, or how he turned him. I just know the night when they showed up and took Emie, Axel was very vengeful toward me. Victor must have told him that my father had left him for dead and saved my life instead. Which I learned wasn't true at all. My father had wanted Joseph to save Axel, and not me. But Joseph seen the good in my heart and knew who I would become. Joseph had chosen to save me that night instead of Axel.

"My father hated Joseph for that. I never learned why, but my father had loved Axel, the first born, and he resented me. All my life, my father treated me like I was a mistake. He favored Curtis over me in all things. Nothing I ever did was good enough." Asher remembered.

"None of that matters now." Asher said to Darryl in the darkness. "All I care about is saving Emie.

"Darryl, I can't wait for you to meet her. She's... she is everything I ever wanted and needed." He told Darryl looking at him.

Darryl listened to Asher's heart. He could see and feel the happiness that was there when he thought and spoke of Emie. He also knew Joseph had made the right decision that night saving Asher's life. Asher truly was a hero.

He put his hand on Asher's shoulder then. "We will find her. We will bring her home. Safe. I promise."

Asher took a deep breath then. He put his arm around Darryl's shoulder and they walked back into the fire house together.

Darryl made his way up to the attic loft where Talia was sleeping. He pulled her body on his as he lay down beside her. He let her sleep till the next morning on his chest all wrapped up in his arms.

Talia stirred sometime after dawn. She could feel the rays of the sunlight heating the attic walls. It warmed her through her cold bones.

She smiled on Darryl's chest knowing he was there holding her.

Darryl felt her stirring, and the smile on her mouth that tickled his chest when her lips moved. He moved his hand into her feathers on her broken wing and marveled at how it had healed in just a few day's time. He started to stroke them. Her feathers were the color of blue flames, and white ash. They were soft like the silk in her robe had been. Now she wore only the firehouse t-shirt that all the rest of the fire heroes wore. It was the one thing that set them apart from the humans down stairs.

Darryl looked into the golden strands of her hair. He followed them down to her arms that were as soft as baby skin. He found there on her arm, a gold chain with a pendant on it. He picked it up then and looked at it. He hadn't noticed it the other night; his mind had been too preoccupied with discovering every inch of her body.

"It's a dew drop. I am the dew that falls from heaven." She whispered to him in a voice that sounded almost like hers.

Darryl tipped up her chin. His finger where he had held the dew drop was moist still. He forgot all about what she had said. Only that she had spoken to him.

Her eyes were no longer black and void less. They were the brilliant blue he had remembered them to be. He watched as she filled her lungs with air and blew out her breath upon his face. He had to close his eyes as the air rushed past him. It was cold like a winter breeze.

"I am healing. And in healing, I will become the angel I once was again. Because of your love, I am becoming whole again Darryl." She whispered sweetly to him against his ear.

When Darryl opened his eyes, he looked upon not just the angel she was, but the woman he had loved his whole life. He cupped her face in his hands and kissed her. He loved her with an urgency that surpassed any feeling he had ever felt.

"Say my name again," he softly asked of her as he rolled her over onto her back. He hadn't heard her speak in so long that just the sound of her voice made him feel more aware of her.

"Darryl." She whispered softly to him, letting his name linger slowly on her lips.

Darryl striped off her t-shirt. He ripped his clothes off his own body and laid his body down onto hers. With one swift thrust he was inside of her body, filling her. With every stroke of his hands he stirred inside of her a rush of passion that flamed inside of her, made her tighten around his member and suck him deeper inside of her. With every rushing emotion, she felt from his stoking of her body, she milked him of his own pleasure, taking it for herself.

Calling out her name with every thrust he found the pleasure his body had longed for all the years he had spent without her. With every kiss, he welcomed her presence inside his life and was reliving in the joyous feelings inside of his heart at their future. He touched her everywhere with his fingers, he took hours finding her pleasure and counted every moment she breathed. He unraveled the strings that made them separate beings as he made love to her and tied them tightly together making them one.

When night fell and he heard the light knock at the attic door, he kissed her lips and her tears. He promised her he would come back to her. "I swear it to you. Once this is over I'll be here, back in your arms Talia."

Talia smiled for him. "I know. I've always known that." She was thinking of the moment he would have died from this world and walked into heavens gates. She had planned on being there, waiting for him.

Darryl stood then and put back on his clothes. Talia watched as he slid his jeans up his hard legs. His body was an ashen gray color unlike the warm pink color of skin. He was solid with a shine of steel that she could feel on her fingers when she touched him. His hair was a little longer then she had ever seen it. He had always had a military crew cut, but now his black hair was fingertip length. Just enough for her to play with.

She would miss the blue in his eyes, but there was something appealing about the blood red color of them now. On the edges of the black center of his eye she could still see streaks of the blue he had lost. She hoped it would stay there if only for her to remember them by.

He noticed she was watching him intently. He could feel her eyes on him, and see the wanderings in her mind. He knew she was blushing without even looking at her. With his arms in the holes of his shirt, before he put it over his head he turned and smiled at her. It brought back a memory from a lifetime ago.

Talia smiled at the memory too.

She had called out to him when he was dressing in the locker room of the high school while he was dressing after a game. She was the journalist for the year book that year. She had snapped a picture of him like that. She had always thought his masculine body was worthy of her worshipping over.

Darryl hadn't thought she was brave enough to put the picture in the year book until she had him sign her own yearbook. She had turned it to the page of his picture and waited for him to sign it for her, biting her lip and grinning at him shamelessly. He had signed it 'Always love me Talia. For I will always love you. Love your hero -Darryl.'

They were both thinking of the memory. He put his t-shirt over his head and pulled it down over his steel hard body as he walked back over to the bed. He leaned down and kissed her lips softly.

Talia could feel the way his loved entered her body and filled all the broken pieces there. She would miss it while he was gone. "Don't forget about me while you are out there playing the hero." She whispered while she winked at him.

Darryl smiled at her and rose to his full height. "Never." He whispered back.

Shelley was sitting in the back of Engine 2 still parked inside the fire house. The men had just returned with it after they had refueled it for their trip to Fort Bragg. She was waiting for everyone who was going on the trip to join her, but she wanted a moment alone to herself.

Curtis had been so preoccupied with Asher that Curtis hadn't spent much time with her at all. Shelley remembered how Emie and Cristina had tried to help her with that particular area, but Curtis' mind just wasn't with her anymore.

Shelley sighed remembering all the times he looked at her lately. Every time his breath caught and seen her face, her lips. Shelley was more in tuned to him now than ever before. She was sure now that she had never felt like this about anyone before. She was more pensive and more relaxed, but ever aware of Curtis' every movement.

His thoughts of her he kept to himself. Shelley would get glimpse of what he saw when he looked at her, but nothing more.

She sighed as she watched the men walking into the bay with the trucks. Asher, Cristina and Curtis would ride along with her in engine 2, while Jordy, Jeremy, Darryl and his men would ride in Engine 1. She had no idea how she was supposed to sit next to Curtis for 10 hours, or longer depending on how they made it through the trip in the dead of winter through the mountains.

Shelley sighed again. Her heart was heavy. She longed for a moment like this to just sit and talk to Curtis. She wondered if he would talk to her on the trip back here with her. If he wanted too.

Curtis was walking up to Engine 2, ready to open the back door as Asher was telling him the route they were going to take. When he opened the back door to put his bags in the back, he noticed Shelley was sitting back there. She was looking at him, not even smiling.

Curtis stopped listening to Asher. He looked at Shelley like he had been doing for days. He felt a pull toward her, but also a push away all at the same time. He shut the door and turned to Asher. He wanted to ask him if he could ride with Darryl, but before the words could cross his lips, he knew she had heard his thoughts. The back door on the other side of the truck creaked open and then closed.

Curtis cussed aloud and told Asher he would be back in a minute. By the time he rounded the other side of the truck, she was gone. He looked out the bay doors and had to feel for her presences. He closed his eyes and seen where she was out by the lake on the pier.

Within a blink of an eye, he was behind her. He placed his arms on either side of the rails around her and watched as her head looked down at the icy water below them. He could see the shiver he caused by appearing behind her on her shoulders. Her thin white blouse she was wearing was falling around her shoulder baring her shoulder and neck to him.

Curtis watched as her long red curly hair blew in the cold winter wind between them. He sighed in a growl at the way it made him feel. He had to hide his thoughts from her. Coward that he was, he didn't want her to know how he felt. He didn't want any of them reading his thoughts. He longed to be normal. He longed to do things the old way. He liked his feeling and thoughts to himself.

And some days, he hated what he had become...

"It's ok if you want to ride with the guys. It doesn't bother me at-" Shelley had to stop talking. Curtis had disappeared again.

Curtis disappeared from behind her. He made her wait for him to reappear though. As stubborn as she was, she was lying about how she felt. And he hated it when she lied.

Shelley had become quiet lately. Joseph had told him on more than one occasion that he needed to talk to her. That Shelley still needed his apology. But Curtis wanted hers first. He could forgive her for all she had done, and he could live with what they had done to him, but he wanted her to admit it now.

He reappeared in front of her. He was standing on one of the rocks in the water. Close enough to touch her on the other side of the rail between them. He could see the wind rush passed her, the way her eyes adjusted to him being in front of her.

His eyes, he had to curse. Whenever they looked at her eyes they always looked down at her lips next. He hated that he did it, but he was drawn to them. Her lips were so full and untouched. They were red out here in the cold. He longed to run his finger across them and warm them.

Shelley was exhausted. She hated all these feelings and not being brave enough to talk to him. When he had cut her off and disappeared, she had almost turned around and left just so she wouldn't be there when he returned.

But he always reappeared so fast, it took her breath away. One second he had left her, and the next he was there. Standing in front of her. His dark brown hair that was just as shaggy as Asher's when it was messed up was moving in the wind. His hard face and lines told her he was thinking and was upset about something, but she couldn't be sure.

When he looked up at her with a crooked smile and looked into her eyes, she couldn't help it when her own lips twitched with a smile when he looked down at her lips.

Curtis leaned forward then, and got in her face. He pulled the back of her hair and made her look up at him. He moved his eyes looking at hers. "I can't sit in the back of that truck with you for days."

"Fine-" she started to say angrily. She watched as his eyes left hers again and looked at her lips. But he disappeared again before she could finish saying anything.

Shelley stomped her foot in anger. "Oh!" She shook her fists at where he had been. She hated the way he made her feel. Angry one second, then madly turned on the next. She hated how he wouldn't let her finish talking either. He drove her crazy.

With one swift movement, she was in his arms again. The next second she was on the beach back home in the warm ocean water with him. He had her body wrapped around his under the water. She looked down and seen they weren't wearing anything. "How did you-"

"Shhh." He hushed her with his finger tip on her lip. His thumb under his finger twitched with an itch to trace her bottom lip. He watched then as his thumb did as he thought. His mouth felt dry and fell open as he watched his thumb do it. His entire body shook with a need he had been denying.

He pulled her into him tighter then closing the distance in the water to their bodies. She was neatly now pressed against him length for length. He knew she would be able to feel his erection, the way his body responded to being alone with her.

Shelley melted into his body under her and felt the closeness of her body up against his and closed her eyes. She wanted to scream at him for what he was doing because if he stopped now she knew she would kill him. She gently licked her lips and touched the tip of his thumb with her tongue. As enticing as it was, she had to break the spell he was creating.

He pushed his thumb into her upper lip then. "Stop talking. Stop thinking. Just listen to me." He told her, looking at her face shamelessly since her eyes were still closed. He pulled his hand away from her face and wrapped his arms around her back.

"I can't sit in the back of that truck with you for days, next to you, and not be this close to you." He pushed his hardness against her then for emphasis. "I can't fight in this war, or let you fight in it, and not-"

Shelley waited. When he couldn't finish his thoughts, she opened her eyes and hollered at him. "And not what?"

Curtis looked in her eyes then. He hadn't wanted her to join the fight with them. He could only pray it would never come to a fight that she wouldn't have to fight.

He told himself then he wouldn't worry about her standing next to him if it came to fight. She would be fine.

But then his mind would picture her being attacked and his heart would break at the thought. He hated it. He hated the feelings he didn't want to have for her. She was so beautiful it made it hard for him not to look at her. She was so careless and hilarious with her words around people that even a simple let down cast at him just the right way made him smile. He couldn't even her hate her the right way because just the sound of her voice played tricks on his mind.

He wanted her to see his need for her. He wanted her to know he needed her to apologize first. He wanted to move past the unease feeling of it all fast so he could just take her and make love to her. So he could be in love with her.

"Tell me you're sorry Shelley."

Shelley felt her anger rise again. He was thinking that much was clear, but he stubbornly wasn't sharing it with her. The kid didn't know how close he was to losing important parts of his body to her that she would do with as she willed. "For what Curtis?"

Curtis starred at her in disbelief again. "Never mind."

He couldn't do it. Every time she said that to him, it angered him that she didn't know. That she couldn't see why he was mad at her. Why he couldn't be with her.

And with that they were back in the back of the fire truck, sitting next to each other, as Asher pulled off the ramp of the fire house.

Shelley looked down at her fully dressed body. She felt for her hair he had somehow wrapped neatly in a bun on her head. She crossed her arms and her leg and looked out the windows. "I hate you."

"I hate you too, darlin." Curtis said to her shamelessly. He grinned to himself in the back window of the fire truck knowing she had days to think about what she couldn't do out there in the water with him. He hoped it haunted her the whole time.

Asher had his arm hanging out the window of his fire truck, holding his smoke. They had finally made it to the mountains in Tennessee. It had been a long hard three-day journey.

Cristina was next to him talking non-stop about Emie, keeping him company. She obviously didn't want him to stop thinking about her, or have a moment to himself. He listened though. He smiled at all their adventures they had shared, and laughed at all the times Emie had done something funny.

Cristina was an excellent storyteller, but she had no idea what she was doing to him. Asher wanted to be alone with his thoughts. He wanted to think about kissing Emie. He wanted to think about holding Emie in his arms. The feel of her body pressed up next to his. The way her hair would curl in his hand when he would run it down one of her curls.

He could feel the pull of her body next to his and longed for her to be here with him. Most of all, he longed for Cristina to stop talking and pretend to be sleeping or something other than talking about Emie.

Curtis leaned forward at Asher's thoughts. "We should stop soon Asher. The men will need some time for themselves."

Asher was grateful for Curtis interrupting Cristina, who agreed with Curtis with a hardy "Oh yes. We should." She even smiled sweetly at him with a knowing smile that said they would finish their conversation later.

When Asher hopped off the truck he thanked Curtis who walked passed him and slugged him in the shoulder saying "Anytime man."

"Will you ride up front when we head back out? Please?" Asher never begged, but he was begging now.

"Not a chance brother." Curtis said as he tucked his hands in his pocket and followed Shelley around the front of the truck to the others.

Asher looked over the ledge of the road that dropped off the side of the mountain they were climbing. They were getting close to Fort Bragg now and he hoped they would not have to make many more detours. Asher wasn't used to following a paper map. Having to stop so he could look at the paper and read between the creases and folds only stirred his irritation more.

Darryl's men were making good time in the daylight hours while they were sitting in the back away from the sunshine, but Asher was starting to have a hard time at night trying to read the maps and keep the trucks on the icy roads.

He stood there looking out over the Great Smoky Mountains and tucked his hands in his pocket for warmth. He found his pack of smokes in his pocket and lit up another one, watching the smoke billow out in front of him.

"Thank you for stopping. Judy and Cain were starting to get restless." Darryl said standing next to him.

Asher nodded his head as he took in another hit of his smoke. He let the burn fill his empty lungs and revealed in the heat of it. "Use the radio anytime you guys need anything." Asher told him, looking at him. Really looking at Darryl again.

Asher had to smile and wonder when he would ever get used to seeing his nephew like this. Darryl's body looked almost death blue in the midnight.

"We should be there soon; it's not much farther now. Once we get out of these mountains and get on the other side of Asheville, we will only be two hundred miles away. Give or take a detour or two." He smiled at Asher who he knew hated detours.

Asher had to shake his head at that. "I just want to get there, man. I want to get that damn plane and finish this."

Darryl knew if it was he that were in Asher's shoes, he would feel the same way. "We are almost there, man." He told Asher as he flicked what was left of his own smoke out over the ledge.

Cain walked up to Darryl then, wagging his tail and sat down next to him. Cain loved to sit like this with Darryl. Like he wanted to be one of the guys and just stare off like Darryl was doing.

Darryl looked down at Cain and then back over out at the mountains. He wondered if it was at all possible for animals to be turned like him as well. The thought of living a life of eternity without someone by his side like Cain, made Darryl wish he could do just that.

"Joseph is the one to ask about such things." Jordy spoke up to Darryl's thoughts and moved by his side.

Darryl looked questioningly at Jordy.

"Those wolves you see roaming around Luna Pier. They are not exactly wolves."

"They are not dogs either." Asher chimed in gruntingly.

Darryl thought about that for a moment. "I'll have to speak with Joseph when I return home then."

Jordy smiled off into the distance of the mountains. There was a new life waiting for all of them when they returned home.

Darryl couldn't wait for this to be over as well. He had a life he was looking forward to with Talia, and he couldn't wait to get started living with her.

Within an hour, they were back on the road again driving through the mountains. Asher drove the rest of the way and stopped just outside of South

Pines, the city before Fort Bragg. They looked like they were driving through an abandoned war zone.

Asher got out and walked around the truck to where Darryl and his men had parked next to him. They looked at the city and were just as surprised as Asher.

"The base is just east of here." Darryl said looking at the map and looking east to where the Army base was. "We shouldn't be able to get to much closer without them seeing us. I hardly doubt they use the check points anymore." He said out loud to nobody particular.

Asher looked at Curtis and Shelley, and then he looked at Jordy and Cristina. He knew they couldn't follow Darryl any further. "You and the guys go on ahead. I don't want to walk in to an ambush and things get out of hand. Radio us when you are ready."

Darryl agreed with him. It would be hard enough to get himself in, let alone five other vampires with him.

Darryl and his men left Asher there in the mountains just outside of North Carolina. They made it safely back to the base and they cleared the roadways as they went so when Asher followed they would be clear for them.

The base was easy to get into, Darryl hid in the back of the tanker just like Asher had planned while his men got them into the base. His men found the commander they had spoke with before, and showed him to the new Darryl.

It was hard at first for the commanders in charge of the base to accept Darryl knowing what vampires had done to the world around them, but seeing the change in Darryl, the man he still was and his desires to see this war over with, that he agreed to help and assist Darryl and his family with the mission they laid out for him.

When Darryl radioed to Asher and the others, he had them brought into the base, plans were made to have Shelley fly a C-130 plane into New York. She would be escorted by fighter jets that would take down the buildings around them and drop bombs on the city until all was destroyed.

After it was all over and Emie was saved, a war would continue to wage between man and the demons. A war that would last for generations. The world man knew, no longer existed. They shared this Earth with more than just demons and vampires. There was an existence of new creatures transforming all around them. A new age had dawned for man.

Darryl was ready to go home though. Before the end, before the new beginning.

Chapter Ten: Saving Emie

New York City

Curtis had doubted Asher's plan, up until he was physically sitting behind Shelley in a passenger seat of a C-130 military plane flying into New York City. He knew his brother was a master mind at planning things out, and he knew what they had to do and what had to be done in order to save Emie. He just worried about all their safety in the process of following it through.

From what he understood of the plans, New York City was swarmed with ancient vampires who sought to seek the extinction of vampires like the Whitby's and sought to destroy the world the humans had built for themselves and take it over. There would be a fight tonight and Curtis was only worried about one person in this plan.

Shelley. She was clouding his mind and she didn't even know it.

Curtis worried about her safety more than anyone else's on this plane and the thought of that ashamed him. His brother was sitting next to Shelley now, giving her directions and instructions. Curtis' nephew Darryl was sitting across from him in the other passenger seat. Why wasn't he worried about their safety the way he worried about hers? He wondered.

Even the Whitby twins who were sitting in the cargo bay under him; why wasn't he even worried about them? Or Emie, he thought to himself as he sat up straighter in his seat. Emie was the reason he had been reunited with his family, the reason he could now be with them. Why wasn't he worried about her?

Curtis didn't understand all the answers to his questions. When he had served as a fire chief on the fire department, he had worried over the safety of all his men during calls. He had always insured all their safety.

Now sitting here behind the woman he had sat next to for the last week in the back of a fire truck, sure of her every breath and movement, he couldn't think of anyone else's safety but hers. He had to make sure she made it out safe tonight. He had to make sure she went back home with him.

He had to make sure...

Curtis leaned forward and spoke to Shelley so only she could hear.

Shelley?

Shelley had been listening to Asher give her specific instructions on where to fly them to, the exact building they were looking for, when she heard Curtis' voice in her mind. She had to search her mind for the voice she heard there to make sure it was Curtis. It was the first time Curtis had ever used his abilities to speak with her like this. Hurriedly she asked him what he needed. What could he possibly need to say to her that no one else could hear? And why now?

Tell me Shelley?

Tell you what Curtis? Shelley said to him worried.

I need you to tell me... Curtis leaned more forward then; he reached his hand beside her pilot's seat and slid his fingers on her bare arm that was resting on the arm rest there. I need you tell me your sorry.

Shelley closed her eyes at his touch. She swallowed a lump she felt in her throat. Feelings that she hadn't felt in ages were welling inside of her.

Whatever it is Curtis, whatever I have done to you that I have wronged, I am so sorry Curtis. Please tell me so I can fix it. This Shelley not only said to him, she showed it to him. She showed him how on bended knee she wanted to be right now. She was very sorry for whatever it was she had done to him.

Curtis closed his eyes then. He wanted to take them both somewhere, anywhere, but they were too close to New York now. He hated himself for waiting so long to talk to her, but he knew now he couldn't let this day pass without doing it. He opened his eyes then and showed her all he had been feeling for years. All the wrong he thought the Whitby's had done to him. And what she had done to him.

If you all had only come to me before this had happened... things would have been so different between us, Shelley.

Shelley listened into Curtis' mind. It was the first time he had ever let her in. Asher was still talking next to her, but she drowned him out and only listened to Curtis.

Why did you wait so long to tell me Curtis? She had to know. She had to know why he had kept this to himself.

Curtis leaned forward more. He knew from the way Asher and Darryl had stilled next to him, that they somehow knew what was going on between Shelley and him, and he didn't care.

At first, I was afraid of you and the others. You took me from the only home I knew and expected me to accept this life like it was a gift of some kind. I wasn't that kind of man Shelley. He told her honestly.

I understand now, the reasons why you all had to do it, but I lost a lot in the process of this all for you guys. I shut you all out right away because of those feelings. I felt safer with them inside of me... I guess. Curtis remembered as he looked out the windows next to him.

But the closer I got to you, the more you made me bend toward you, I couldn't help the way I started to feel, that anger that came. But then, other feelings for you started, and it only fueled my anger at all the wrong times.

Shelley chuckled at that. It was always at the wrong times.

I have been torn for so long Shelley. Curtis told her lowering his head down. I don't want to be like this anymore. It's not me.

Why now? Why are you waiting till right now to tell me all of this? She asked him, very unsure about his honesty.

Curtis looked up then at the back of her seat. He could see her sitting there in his mind. He had memorized Shelley from the perfect red strands in her curly hair that reminded him of hot flames, to her cute little stubby toes she loved to paint. He thought about all the things he had been thinking about in the back of the fire truck.

Curtis had to chuckle and shake his head at all his thoughts he had in the back of the fire truck. He had fallen in love with her in the back of his fire truck.

He let her see it. He let her see every dream he had of them living together for the rest of their lives.

For the first time in Shelley's existence, she felt tears running down her cheeks. She had wanted everything Curtis was dreaming about her whole life. Everything he was seeing, from loving her, to holding her, to keeping her safe beside him, to living; it was everything she had ever wanted, all she had ever hoped for was there in his dreams with her. She had to look back down at the controls and hold on tighter to the plane to bring her back to reality.

I can't go back to living like I have been Shelley after this is all over. I can't go back to living the life I had once lived alone before you came into my life either. I want you Shelley. I want to spend the rest of my life with you.

No matter what happens tonight, you have to make it back home with me.

Shelley wiped away the tears that were blinding her now. She sat up a little taller and thought about all the witty comebacks she would normally be saying to this man right now. Like "Why the hell should I?" or "Aren't you going to ask me what I want?"

But she didn't want to say any of them. She had to look out in front of her at the city that was coming into view. She knew what laid in wait for them all there. She knew Emie was there waiting to be rescued. But all she wanted to do was get out of her seat and melt into the arms of Curtis.

Oh I will. Because when this is all over, I swear it to you; I am going to make you pay for this in ways that should scare the hell out of you.

Curtis laughed out loud to her comment and sat back in his seat. He looked at Darryl and realized no one else had heard what she had said and he almost felt awkward about it, but he loved this woman. He looked back at the seat Shelley was sitting in shaking his head at her.

I just might let you Darlin.

Shelley smiled into the night in front of her and tried to focus on the route while trying not to think of the ways she was going to make him pay for all he had put her through for the rest of their lives.

She failed, miserably.

Asher coughed next to her. "If I can have your attention please, can we focus on the big building in front of you you're about to miss?"

"Oh, that one?" Shelley asked Asher, pointing at the building that stood taller than the rest in the skyline of New York City. She smiled at him jokingly and winked.

Asher smirked over at her. "Yes." Then he looked back at Curtis rolling his eyes.

Darryl edged closer to the middle isle and looked out the window to where the building stood they were all about to fly into. He noticed Jordy and

Jeremy had come up into the cockpit with them also to take a peak.

Curtis looked over at every one and went over the plans one more time. "Everyone needs to be holding onto me when we get closer. Do not let go of me until I tell you to."

The plan was for Shelley to put the plane on autopilot once they were in range and then for Curtis to take them all to the road in front of the building before the plane crashed into the building.

Curtis would then take Asher above the crash site into the building and try to attempt to land on the right floor or least as close to Emie as he could, followed by Jordy. Once Asher or Jordy reached Emie, Curtis would then take her and Shelley back home before any fight broke out. Then Curtis would take everyone else back one by one until everyone was home safe.

Asher's plan was to stay as long as he could until he found Victor and Axel. He wasn't leaving until both men were destroyed, until he had set both men on fire.

Curtis looked around the seat to Shelley and watched her as she looked at the building. He waited for her to say the words that auto pilot was on, and then he grabbed Shelley and held onto everyone in the plane as quickly as he could and landed them all on the road safely below the plane.

Asher looked up once his feet were firmly placed on the road. He watched as the plane flew across the sky and he followed its path down the road until it hit its target. Freedom washed over him. He could go and find Emie now.

He looked back at Curtis then. "Now Curtis!"

Curtis looked up. He had been watching too. He looked back at Shelley and winked at her, and then he looked at Darryl. "Keep her safe Darryl." He said as he reached for Asher and disappeared into the building where Emie was.

Darryl stood in the midst of where his uncles had just been standing. It all felt like they were back in high school again scheming and planning with Asher.

Shelley heard in Darryl's mind a tale he was thinking about. She looked at Darryl then as they started walking toward the trade center. "Tell me what you are thinking about?" she asked.

Darryl smiled over at her. "Ah, I was just remembering high school." Darryl thought as he looked at the burned, broken city around them.

"Asher and Curtis had just lost their first game of their last season in football. They were so mad. It was this other guy's fault entirely you see." He said looking over at Shelley. "He had fumbled the ball in the last few seconds of the game. The turn over cost us the game. The other team ran the ball all the way for a touchdown.

"Asher made plans over the weekend to pay him back for it. We planned all weekend what we were going to do." Darryl laughed at the memories.

"On Monday morning when everyone else was in the school, he and Curtis tipped the guys car over on its side and left it there like that until the end of the day."

Shelley laughed a little too at the thought. Asher and Curtis were such big guys. She could just see them out in parking lot doing something like that at the high school. "Sounds like a lot of damage to a guy's wallet over just a game."

"You're not a guy or on a football team." Darryl said over to her as they rounded the last corner. He waited for the building to come into view then as he spoke to her. "You wouldn't understand.

"He understood though, and knew the penalty for it was coming. Asher and Curtis paid for the tow truck and some of the damages, plus they got suspended. The guy learned to never fumble the ball ever again though. He's in the pros now. Asher and Curtis never played football again after that year, but they always go to his games in Detroit."

Shelley had to wonder about the family she was getting to know. She was starting to like them more and more every day.

Darryl was looking at the world trade center that was looming eerily in the night sky above them. There was smoking rolling out of the building above them and fire was raining all around them along with debris. It was like everything they had watched on TV so many years ago, just different this time around.

This time around, Darryl knew why it was happening. He had learned quickly that Victor was responsible for it all. Victor had wanted Emie and thought he could get to her through Asher. Darryl shook his head at the thought of it all. Victor and his army were going to lose tonight and pay for their sins.

When he heard the screeching above him, he knew it was time for Curtis to hurry up and finish the plans. Shelley was not safe out here unguarded. If things came to a fight; he knew the demons would tear her apart.

Darryl reached for Shelley just as one above them screeched loudly and dove right for Shelley. He wrapped her in his arms and shielded her with his steel armored body.

Flexing his arms for the first time since he had been changed, he reached up for the demon before it could swipe its claws at him. He pulled hard on the arm of its wing and ripped it clean off its body and sent the demon spiraling back up into the air as far as he could throw it.

He smiled at his handy work. It was the first time he had been able to have a good fight with one of the demons since the last time he had been here in New York.

Shelley grinned back at Darryl who was still holding onto the demon's arm. "Are you going to keep that as a souvenir tough guy?"

Darryl smiled over at her as he spun her around in a swift dance move and winked at her. "I just might."

Within seconds, in a blink of an eye, Shelley was gone. Darryl had watched her happier than he had ever seen her as he twirled her around watching her long shiny red curly hair spin with her. Then Curtis was behind her with his arms wrapped around her whispering something in her ear as he winked over at Darryl and left with her.

Darryl saluted Curtis before he disappeared and found himself grinning at the happy couple. He shook his head and stuffed his hands in his pocket laughing.

He knew how Curtis felt right now. Darryl couldn't wait to get back home to his own love of his life.

He looked back up at the building in front of him and saw all the demons floating above it like a swarm of angry birds. A hand clapped him on the shoulder pulling him out of his daze.

Darryl had heard the chopper land behind him some time ago when he had been talking to Shelley and knew his men were on their way over to him. He was grateful they were here with him tonight. He was going to need all the help he could get keeping the demons out of the tower so Asher and Curtis could get everyone out safe and back home before a fight broke out.

"Hey man." Bartley said to him as the others started firing on the demons above them.

"Hey Bartley. It's good to see you man." They watched as the choppers above them started firing on the demons too, and hunched over as the fighter jets dropped bombs on the buildings around them.

New York City was being lit up with fire and buildings were exploding around them. Vampires and demons were being picked off one by one tonight. They could feel the familiar sounds of war around them and it only sharpened their skills for battle.

"They won't know what hit them." Bartley said to Darryl with a smile after the last bomb hit behind them.

"Come on. We've got work to do." Darryl said to his men as they ran into the tower in front of them.

Darryl directed Johnny and Jimmy to stay outside with Pat and keep anyone or anything from entering on the ground floor. He took Bartley with him on the inside. With guns at the ready, Bartley stayed by his side as they walked into the corridor.

Darryl noticed the rush of men in front of them. They didn't give a second look at Darryl sensing immediately that he was a vampire like them. They were all too busy trying to figure out what their leaders wanted them to do now that a plane had crashed into the building.

Darryl listened and watched as Victor, the man Asher was looking for, directed the men where to go. Darryl watched as realization hit Victor, the moment Victor realized Darryl and Asher were together. The man Darryl knew now was Asher's brother, pointed toward Darryl and Victor smiled with a determination that sickened both Bartley and himself.

Darryl reached his hand back and stayed Bartley. "Go back out with the guys, I got this." He sensed when Bartley hesitated but he knew Bartley would obey his command without question.

Darryl then watched as the room went silently still. No one was moving. It scared the hell out of him. Even Victor, noticed it all. He was waving his hand in front of Axel trying to get his attention. But then, like everyone else, Victor, too, froze.

Cristina flew through the room and out the front doors.

I stopped time for you. Take as long as you need. She whispered to him.

I'll need Axel though, if you don't mind. Darryl said, nodding at the bat that flew past him. He was grateful for her being here.

"Well, well. If it isn't my long-lost nephew. We've been looking for you." Axel said in a voice that sounded as angelic as it did demonic. He made his way over to Darryl and stopped just out of his reach.

Darryl spent little time thinking about that. He summoned Asher to hurry, he knew there was going to be a fight soon. But he was still shocked by the way all the vamps in the room including Victor were standing stark still.

Darryl let out a growl the closer Axel got.

In a burst of what felt like electric on his skin, he felt the terrible tremble that filled his body and shook him. He hated that feeling. That old feeling he used to get that always took him by surprise and tried his damndest not to think about it now. He couldn't think of anything but his enemy now. Axel.

"I take it you met the Whitby's, looking at the way you've changed and are looking at me now." He waited for Darryl to acknowledge him.

"Good. That means they're here. I thought that was them who flew that big ol plane into the building." Axel said winking at him sheepishly.

Axel started to taunt Darryl by trying to circle around him while he spoke. "As you probably learned from the Whitby's, your uncle and I were brothers. Watching him die and taking Emie from him was pure pleasure for me."

Darryl realized Axel thought Asher was dead then. They had tried to kill Asher when they took Emie, but they had failed. Darryl didn't let Axel see it on his face that he was wrong. He thought to himself with a smile though, that Victor was in for the surprise of his life.

"It's a pity that you didn't die in that accident thirteen years ago."

Rage. Pure, white hot rage filled Darryl from his heart to his soul. He tried not to think about the accident that had taken Talia's life. He begged the thoughts to stop just long enough to kill Axel. He waited though, and let Axel finish talking. He knew how to defeat an enemy, and he was just waiting for the right second to kill this man.

"I tried like hell to make sure you did. See, Victor sent me to kill you too, to make sure you didn't live to see this day." Axel grinned wickedly at Darryl trying to bait him. "Who knew your girlfriend was brave enough to fight me for you though, right?"

Darryl stood stark still then. What did he just say?

"Yeah, that's right. She braved the sun's fire to attack me. You didn't know, did you, you lucky bastard? That you were entertaining an angel in your bed? But you see, like Asher, I, too, have the power over fire." He lifted his middle finger to make his point and his finger lit with a flame like a lighter. "I made sure she died quickly. But not before she could save your pathetic life."

Darryl stood up taller then. He looked in the eyes of the man he required and for the first time he felt what Joseph and everyone else had talked about. There were some men in this world that God required their life. And Darryl was the man for the job. He could see it in his mind like a script. This man was going to die by his hands and his hands alone.

"You thought you could stop us all these years, didn't you? Even now, I can see it in your eyes. But

I've been hunting you and her for so long." Axel took a deep breath and breathed in the scent of Darryl trying to coax him more. "It will be a pleasure now to watch you die slowly like I watched her die when I had her cut down from heaven's realm."

In a flash, Axel touched Darryl's arm. He looked back then at Darryl astonished. He had tried to set Darryl on fire, but Darryl skin was made of steel. Steel!

Darryl smiled wickedly still at Axel. Fire couldn't touch him, and Axel couldn't kill him. He hadn't even flinched when Axel had grabbed his arm. "How's it feel?"

Axel looked at him questioningly, and it made Darryl laugh.

Darryl grabbed Axel by the neck and squeezed until he felt his neck stretching and tearing. He stopped long enough to bore down into Axel's eyes and say one last thing.

"How does it feel to know you've been outwitted, out played? How's it feel," Darryl asked him again, lifting him off the ground, "to know YOU are gonna die?"

Darryl let him see it in his eyes. He watched as the man struggled, watched as he tried to grab at Darryl's hand. Nothing Axel did to fight Darryl could be done. Darryl was stronger, wiser, and a better man than Axel ever was.

Axel's skin was melting above Darryl's hand from the steel.

Darryl reached his other hand up and grabbed Axle's head. He twisted and tore Axle's head off his body. He turned the man's head around and watched as Axel cried out in agony. Darryl, the soldier he was, felt the excitement over the win of killing Axel.

Asher was by his side then. All the other vampires in the room had been set on fire at his entrance. There was just one more left that Asher required, but first he wanted to help his nephew.

Darryl introduced the head of Axel who was barley still alive to Asher who had just bumped him on the shoulder to let him know he was there.

Asher grinned at Axel and lit his own finger. "Your turn." Asher laughed then out loud. "Oh. By the way," he said angrily to Axel. "Emie's mine!"

Darryl tossed Axel's head to Asher and watched as Asher lit it and tossed it on Axel's body that caught fire also. He nodded at Asher in thanks then as they bumped fists.

Asher smirked at Darryl. "Go, have fun with your men. I got Victor."

Darryl noticed over by the main counter that Victor was watching them in stunned silence. He nodded and saluted to Asher and walked back out of the building with a victorious smile on his face.

Chapter Eleven: Saving Shelley

Shelley looked around the fire house for Curtis after he had left her to go and rescue Asher but he still wasn't back yet. She knew Emie was safe and sound in her new room now. She could hear her mind wandering around her new room waiting for Asher's return. Shelley was happy for her friend. Emie deserved the happy ending Asher was about to give her.

Shelley looked around some more and waited. Waiting for what, she wasn't quite sure of. She just found herself standing there wrapped up in her own lonely arms looking at where the fire trucks should have been. The bay was empty now. It looked as empty as she felt.

She found Joseph and spoke with him about Talia. She had learned that Talia was missing, but Joseph assured her that Talia was safe also. With that, Shelley again began to wonder what she was supposed to do with herself.

She couldn't go home now. She wasn't safe there anymore alone. This made her laugh at herself. After two hundred years here in the United States living alone on her own, now she wasn't safe. She'd seen many wars here. Enough to last her a lifetime.

Shelley nervously curled a finger through one of her curls hanging down on her arm. She always hated feeling like this.

All the doors had been closed for the safety of those who were still inside. They were welded shut with reinforced steel. She knew the sun was rising soon, so going for a walk outside was out of the question.

Shelley sighed to herself and walked into the radio room behind her. It was the only room in the firehouse that was empty at the moment. Sitting in the desk chair she looked around the room.

The computer was shut down and the screen was dark. The only light in the room was the flashing green lights coming from the radios being charged for the fire fighters should they need them. Shelley sat back in the chair and turned on the computer.

There was no longer internet to check her emails with any longer, which meant checking her social media account wasn't going to happen either. Shelley had lost touch with everyone she knew in just a few month's time. Sometimes she would wonder about her distant friends and wondered what they were all doing now. Were they trying to do the same things the Whitby's were doing to save the world?

Shelley doubted that. Most of her friends were loners like her. They lived on their own out of society. It was easier that way she told herself remembering how it had been for her until she had met the Whitby's.

Shelley leaned forward when the computer came to life. She knew her way around a computer with ease, and was able to get into the gallery of pictures the fire fighters had taken over the years. She clicked on the first folder she could find titled "2009 old pics" and started going down the endless pictures of old fire scenes. She wasn't surprised when she found pictures of Curtis. In a lot of the pictures he wasn't acting or putting on a show, he was fully involved and working hard.

She had to move past a lot of the heart wrenching pictures of families and their homes on fire. Every accident scene she seen just made her scroll faster.

She wondered how all of these brave men and women do this for a living. She understood their passion for it the more she looked at the pictures. The people in the pictures needed saving, and the Stone boys were the men for the job, she told herself.

They weren't just working in the pictures that she seen playing out before her like a video feed. They were saving lives. Trying to save people's homes and places of business from being destroyed.

She sat back at one picture and had to cover the horror she seen there. Curtis and Asher were crawling out of a burning window, their names she could clearly read on the backs of their jackets. Black, hot, white smoke along with red and orange flames was billowing around them as they escaped.

"I wonder how they got out of that room unscathed?" she wondered aloud, looking more at the picture.

"We weren't climbing out Darlin, we were climbing in."

Shelley knew it was Curtis without even looking at him. But he had made her jump when he appeared in the chair behind her. He was resting his arms on the arms of her chair.

Shelley looked back at him them. "Why would you climb into those hell fires in that house?"

"Cause that's what we do." He explained. "Well, that's what I 'did'. I don't think I will be running into any burning buildings now." He jested down at her. "I'll just tell everyone else what do from now on." He grinned at her. "I'd rather not die in flames again."

Shelley turned her chair around then to face him. "Promise me you won't or this thing…" She pointed to the two of them. "Whatever this thing is." She said smiling bashfully up at him. "It's not gonna work if you don't understand the rules."

"Oh, this thing." He said pointing to her and him like she had done. "It has rules now?"

Shelley thought about that. He was grinning at her now like he was happy. Happier then she had seen him in a long time.

"Yes." She said softly to him. She couldn't help herself. She had to look at his lips. They were sensually parted from the last word he had spoken.

"What's the first rule then?" He asked sheepishly seeing the way her eyes were looking at his lips. It stirred a desire deep inside of him. He had to curl his toes in his boots like claws that were reaching for her body. His hands itched with the need to be in her hair again. To feel her hair tickle the sides of his arm as he held it in his hand.

Shelley cocked her head and thought carefully about that. She spun the chair back around and faced the computer. "First, no more of this 'fire hero' shit." She told him moving her hand toward the computer.

"Ah, I see." Curtis whispered in her ear as he leaned in closer behind her. He placed his arms back on the chairs arms like before, but this time he placed his hands on her waist and pulled her chair back against him.

Shelley breathed in a deep breath. She could smell Curtis and marveled at the smell in the fire house that matched the smell of Curtis. Fire was in his blood just like it was in Asher's.

"What's rule number two then?" He whispered again closer to her ear this time. He waited till she shivered then he said, "Tell me Shelley."

Shelley tried not to shiver. She really did. But the way his breath lingered there on her skin made her own toes curl. "No more disappearing acts." She said aloud to him breathlessly.

Curtis grinned wickedly then. He knew she could read his thoughts and knew she was going to be upset about the one rule he couldn't obey.

"Well, I want one of my own then."

Shelley almost blurted out "Anything" until she realized he was teasing her. "What it is?" she asked seductively.

Curtis traced the back of her ear with his nose. He knew he was driving her crazy when he felt her body shiver. "No more mind reading when we are together."

Shelley closed her eyes and knew that was impossible. He started tracing her neck with his nose breathing her in then and she wasn't able to respond to him.

"Promise?" Curtis stopped teasing her, but he didn't move an inch away from her either.

"I'll do what I can." Her body trembled then. She wanted more of what he was doing and didn't want him to stop. She felt his smile on her neck, and knew he would accept at least that.

Curtis started kissing Shelley's neck slowly. He had never kissed her before. He wondered how long it would take her to turn around and kiss him fully.

When she did, he raised his finger up to her lips. "Ah, ah, ah. You promised no mind reading."

"That's not fair Curtis!" She demanded.

Curtis sat back in his chair angrily. "Fine."

Shelley waited for the moment she knew would break her heart. Any time in the past when Curtis said that, he would always disappear. She almost started pleading right then and there for forgiveness.

In a blink of an eye, this time, he took her with him. One second she was sitting in the radio room in Luna Pier. The next she was in her bed at home in Florida.

Shelley was laying flat on her back, her arms wrapped neatly around Curtis' neck. She closed her eyes then and shook head in laughter.

"Come on, admit it. You like it." Curtis asked her with a laughing grin of his own as he looked tenderly down at her.

Shelley opened her eyes only to see the smile on Curtis' face that made her heart wrench.

Shelley had to admit it though. She was very impressed by his ability, irritating as it was. She looked down though and noticed something.

"No clothes?" she questioned up at him, even though she already knew the answer.

Curtis quirked a grin down at her and looked down between them. Her perfect breasts were pressed against his chest. He lay between her legs nestled up into her. "No." he whispered softly to her.

Shelley sighed and looked up into his face. Curtis had smile lines around his eyes and his lips. Curtis was in his thirties and had lived a long happy life before her she could tell. It was one of the things she loved about him. The way he just wanted to be happy and playful all the time.

She made a mental note to make sure he was always happy like this. Always smiling. She liked him better that way.

"You don't play fair Darlin."

"Oh really?" Curtis questioned her. "I seem to remember a time when you liked to make sure I wasn't wearing any clothes so you could have your way with me." Curtis mentioned to her raising an eyebrow.

Shelley grinned back at him. She knew she would be blushing if she could.

She had done just that to him in the beginning trying to get his attention when he would reappear after disappearing from her during training. She would wrap him in steel chains so he couldn't do it again when he came back, as quickly as she could and then she would strip him naked just because she could as a show of strength against him.

"I must admit, I did it more out of curiosity then punishment." She told him honestly.

This surprised Curtis. "Really? Well then." He asked while he ran his thumb across her lips. "Did you like it Shelley?"

Shelley closed her eyes. She loved when Curtis did this to her. She loved how he said her name like that whenever he spoke to her and was able to command control over her. No one had ever been capable of it. Well, no one had ever had the balls to do it to her, she thought off handedly. But Curtis, she told herself, he knew what he was doing, and she loved it.

Curtis ran his hand up into her hand behind her ear when she didn't answer him right away and tugged on her hair there. He swiftly moved his mouth to her neck and bared his fang there against her skin. He dragged his upper fangs along her skin there sending chills all throughout her body.

He relished in the moan that broke from her lips. When he reached the bottom of her earlobe he licked behind it and sucked it into his mouth making her twist in sweet pleasure.

"Answer me Shelley!" He commanded of her, stopping and pulling on her hair. "Did you like it?" This last he said softly in almost a whisper as he looked into her eyes at that question and demanded an answer.

She could feel his command unlike any time before. She suddenly wondered if this was a new ability or just something he had learned from Joseph. Whatever it was, she sinfully craved it.

"Hell yeah." She said aloud more to her thoughts than his question. "You could say I found a few things that captivated my attention."

Shelley took her eyes off Curtis' face that was proud of her answer to let them linger on his bare chest. She traced the outline of his peck with a fingertip. "I have always enjoyed looking at the male form. My eyes," She told him, raising her own back up to his, "have always been drawn to it shamelessly." Shelley smiled then; she was picturing all the wonderful things she had discovered about Curtis' body, from his tight well-muscled, powerful thighs, to the strawberry birthmark patch on his lower back just above the clef in his buttocks that were just as tight and powerful as his thighs. He probably didn't even know the birthmark was there she told herself quietly.

Curtis growled at her then as he drank in her lovely face. "God, I can't get enough of you." he said pressing his manhood up closer to the inside of her. He slid between her lips rubbing on her clit making her body shiver with every movement.

Shelley was dying now. He still hadn't kissed her yet. Her body was being overpowered by the need of it. She could feel the tremble on her lips and taste it in her mouth the way her venom dripped on her tongue and made her salivate. Her eyes were so drawn to his lips she couldn't stop looking at them and licking her own lips. She wanted his kiss. She needed it.

Shelley watched as his lips opened in a smile that turned into a wide grin. When she looked up into his eyes she could see he was laughing at her. "What?" She questioned him, unable to hide her own smile.

"Now who's looking at whose lips?" He nodded in question to her while his eyes bore into her for an answer.

Shelley took in a deep breath then and hollered at him. "Will you just kiss me already? Damn you!"

Curtis placed his hands on either side of her and lifted her up a little. "Ah ha!" he exclaimed playfully. "Wait till I tell Jordy and Jeremy! The great and powerful Shell-"

Shelley cut him off before he could finish his thoughts with a kiss. Shelley never begged! And now she was the one who could say she kissed him first.

Ha! She told his mind. I got you first.

Curtis didn't care. He had to take command of the kiss. It had nothing to do with being a man; it had nothing to do with having control, or being prideful. It was pure, lustful, desire that took over him.

He smiled into her kiss at first yes, how couldn't he? He had made her beg, and it felt amazing to say the least. But now, with her body under his while he was kissing her, open to his touch, willing and accepting his every movement; was a kind of heaven he had never experienced before.

Curtis had his share of women in his lifetime, but he had never dreamed of having a woman as pure and real as Shelley. She was the first woman he had met that awakened his soul with just her laughter. That could look at him with those eyes and speak to him in ways he never thought possible.

Shelley was fiery; she was smoking hot in his firefighter mind. He loved the way her hair was the color of red hot flames, that her creamy white alabaster skin reminded him of hot smoke. He desired her body in ways that made every muscle in his body flex with the need to grab and hold on to her.

He found himself in an embarrassingly constant state of passion and desire when he was around her. Now that she was finally under him, kissing him, he could finally set free the raw need he had been feeling for her for so long. Curtis held onto the back of her hair in his fist and kissed her the ways Shelley deserved to be kissed.

Shelley could feel now the control he had over her. She knew now what it was she had been drawn to all this time. Curtis had a power he didn't know he had. She could feel it in her head where he was holding onto her the way it stirred in her skin and made her hair raise to a chilling temperature.

She could feel it in the muscles of her neck when he kissed her there. Curtis could not only command her heart and mind; he had the perfect ability to make her body feel everything he wanted her to feel.

The lower his kisses went down her body, the more her body rose off the bed like he was kissing her from the inside out. His great command was so powerful Shelley found herself calling out to him in one blissful moment after another.

Curtis dug his fingertips into her body as he dragged them down her skin. He pinched her nipples and smiled wickedly at her when she moaned as he dragged his finger around and around her breast teasing her. He returned his lips to hers and kissed her lips hard and wildly.

When Curtis grabbed the back of her hair again, she could see he had a question in his mind and hated him for stopping. She even growled at him when he did. He pulled her head against the pillow and tipped her face up to his. She read the desire there in his mind and was well pleased with it.

Shelley left her mouth opened to him while he pulled on her hair and Curtis saw her fangs that were dripping. Her lips were red and swollen from his endless kissing of her lips. He longed to kiss her for so long he couldn't stop doing it now. With his growing desire that was only building dangerously, his cock was lying between her lower folded lips, he needed to enter her and stop all this foolish wanting.

But first, he couldn't just take her without knowing something first. "I have to know Shelley. I can't just continue like this and not know."

Shelley felt her desire grow to a painful degree. She raised her leg and ran the side of her thigh up his to his hip. She needed him to kiss her again. "What Curtis?"

Curtis looked down into her eyes then. He looked deeper then and almost couldn't believe the way he did it. He reached further and found the source he was looking for. He found her wanting soul. He found the depths of her heart, the emotional state of her being. And when he found it, he found himself there.

Inside of Shelley's mind, her heart and soul, inside of the very place of her being that made Shelley; he found himself, and marveled at it.

"Is this love?" he questioned her.

Shelley felt her whole world come crashing down. No one had ever seen inside of her. She had kept herself locked up so tightly, so firmly shut, that no one could ever open her up. But here he was. The man that she craved, the man she had to have, he was deeper inside of her than any one had ever been. She was so awed by it she almost couldn't believe it.

For one heartbreaking second, Shelley almost threw it all away. With the quickness of time it took to breath in one breath, she almost pushed him away.

But then he said, commandingly, "Tell me Shelley?"

And with that, she couldn't lie to him. She couldn't hide from him. She had to tell him.

"Yes." And then she said, slowly, "I love you Curtis." Because she had never ever had any one to love before and because she only wanted to love him. No one else but him.

Curtis almost lost control of it for a moment. He couldn't believe what she had just shared. No one had ever loved her. And she had never loved anyone because of it.

It broke him. It hurt him. Because he loved her.

Curtis looked down at the woman in his arms. Shelley. He looked at her face, her eyes, her lips, and her body; he could see under him without looking at it because he had already memorized it. Her hair, her fingers, her legs, her toes; every inch of this woman he loved.

Curtis unraveled his mind and gave up the control he always tried to keep over his mind to block her out with. He gave it to her by looking in her eyes.

He showed her everything there. And he would never take it back from her.

Shelley held onto his face while she looked into Curtis' soul. She hungrily drank from his mind like he was saving her. Her eyes dripped with tears that Shelley had never shed before. He loved her. She could see it. He didn't have to say it. She, could see it. It was the sweetest gift anyone could ever have given her.

When her heart finally had its fill of its need, she came back into reality and seen the waiting smile there on Curtis' lips. He was brushing away the tears that were falling off her cheeks. Shelley closed her eyes then and relished in the touch of him. She needed it.

And with that, Curtis had his answer. He didn't have to hold back any longer. Shelley was his. All he had to do now was sink himself inside her and make love to her forever.

And that's just what he did.

Chapter Twelve: Saving Darryl

Joseph was waiting on the roof of the Luna Pier Fire House for Darryl. It was midnight now and every one of his family members had made it home safely a few days ago because of Darryl and his men.

He sat there in the midnight hours waiting for the man he owed his life to. The man who helped save his little sister Emie.

He didn't know when he would see Emie again, she was lost in her new room with Asher, and Joseph knew it would be days before he got to see her. Just knowing she was home though, safe, was all that mattered to him.

Joseph turned his head at the sound of the door opening behind him. Darryl was walking out here to see him. Joseph took a deep breath of the cold midnight air. He looked down at his hands pondering. He knew what he was about to say to Darryl was going to change everything.

"Jordy said you wanted to see me?" Darryl said as he took a seat on the ledge next to Joseph and looked out over the lake in the darkness. The stars in the darkness of the heaven above them twinkled unlike anything he had ever seen before.

"I need to say thank you to you Darryl. I owe you my life for saving her."

Darryl nodded to Joseph in acceptance and took in his surroundings of home here in Luna Pier and was thankful that this long journey of war he had been on for so long had finally ended.

All Darryl wanted to do for a long time was just sit here like this in his home and be content, quiet and alone for the rest of his life.

Joseph sighed and looked down at his hands again. "The war you seek to run away from Darryl has just begun."

"I know." Darryl really didn't care anymore about it. "My place is here though. Home. I'm never leaving again Joseph. I've been gone for too long."

Joseph looked up at the stars like Darryl was doing. He listened to Darryl's mind, thinking about other things then duty and honor and glory. Darryl wanted to be here with his family, those he loved.

It had taken Darryl a few days longer to get back home. He had to help his men get back safely to Fort Bragg. It was a promise Darryl had made them that when Emie was safely back home and their mission was over, they could take their leave and try to return back to their own homes. To their own families.

Once he had seen them back to the base in Fort Bragg, he had met up with Curtis and Jordy who helped him drive back the fire trucks to Luna Pier.

Darryl started thinking of Talia then. He wanted this meeting with Joseph to be over so he could go to her.

Joseph looked over at Darryl then trying not to breathe.

"What?" Darryl questioned Joseph with a sense of unease. "Where is she Joseph?" He could see in Joseph's mind then. Something wasn't what it should be.

Darryl almost stood then. He put both hands on his knees and could see in Joseph something had happened to her.

Joseph took another steadying breath and prayed for strength. Darryl may be new to this life, but he knew Darryl could crush him if so wished to right now. "Not too long after you left, she finished healing Darryl. The love between her family and yours, mixed with the love you continued to feel for her everyday finally made her whole again."

Darryl sat there next to him, trying to listen to Joseph, but he was ready to run. Ready to find her. Something inside of him told him she wasn't here anymore, and that scared the hell out of him.

"One day she was here, laughing and talking, sharing things with all of us we never knew about. The next day, she was this beautiful angel again.

Joseph bowed his head down lower this time. He knew this next blow was going to get him killed by Darryl. He braced himself so he could escape if need be.

"Where is she Joseph?" Darryl asked Joseph point blankly. Darryl tried to sit there and be patient. He was really trying hard. But Joseph was trying his patience.

Joseph put his hands together then and looked over at Darryl. "She was sitting up here, just like this, a few days ago. I could see her from downstairs and I knew she was ok. She was just up here daydreaming.

"And then she thought of something that scared her. And she just disappeared."

"Where the hell did she go?" Darryl yelled, standing to his full height.

When Darryl stood ready to strangle the life out of Joseph, Joseph stood before him and placed up his hands in surrender. "I don't know Darryl!"

"Well what the hell was she thinking about then?" This, he begged of Joseph. Anything that could give him a clue of where she was, where she had went.

"I don't know! What happened a few days ago?" Joseph questioned him unsure of what to do to help him.

Darryl placed both of his hands in his hair in frustration. Then he started to pace. He searched through his mind back through the last couple of days, and then he remembered. He stopped dead in his tracks then.

The fight with Axel.

"Damn it all!" he said aloud to himself. He remembered that feeling he had right before the fight with Axel. It was her. That feeling he used to get, it was why he had felt it again then. She had been beside him again. She had also heard everything Axel had said, he thought shaking his head.

He looked back up at the heavens then and placed his hands on his hips frustrated.

She must have seen or felt the fight somehow, he thought to himself. What he didn't understand though was what would she have done if she knew he was in danger?

And then he knew. He knew!

She had gone back to heaven and went back to being his guardian again. It was what she had told him he had done after she had died the first time.

Darryl rounded on Joseph then ready to strangle more information out of him.

"I didn't make this decision Darryl. You will have to take it up with a higher power." Joseph watched as a torn Darryl was standing before him, exasperated but ready for battle, ready to tear someone to shreds. He begged Darryl though then. It wasn't his fault what Talia had done, and he made Darryl understand it.

Darryl growled inside himself at Joseph and turned around slamming his hands down on the ledge in front of them. No, Joseph didn't understand this, he told himself.

She was promised to him!

"How the hell do I get her back Joseph?" This he said looking back Joseph.

"I don't honestly know Darryl." Joseph said to him again in surrender.

Darryl looked at Joseph and studied him. He looked at the man who resembled his brothers Darryl had just spent weeks with. He could see the goodness in him the way he could Joseph's brothers. He looked away knowing Joseph was telling him the truth. Knowing Joseph honestly didn't know how to handle this.

Darryl jumped over the edge of the fire house then.

Joseph looked down and watched Darryl land on the ramp of the bay with the ease of a man on a mission. "Where are you going Darryl?" He shouted after him.

Darryl looked over to the pier and the Lighthouse that stood vigilantly at the end of the road over the lake. "I'm going to pray." He told Joseph as he walked away.

He was going to find God again. He needed answers. Answers he was afraid to find.

Again.

Joseph watched as Darryl left and headed over to the beach. "Damn it." He said under his breath as he walked away from the ledge and headed back into the fire house.

While he walked down the steps in the house back into the main meeting hall, he headed back over to the bay where Jeremy and Jordy were loading the fire trucks back into. He stood there, hands in his pockets, and he summoned out to his family to join him in the bay.

When Jeremy and Jordy finished unloading the trucks, he told them to wait until Asher and Emie got there before he could explain what he needed.

Joseph knew he was going to need Emie's help with Darryl. Darryl was on a mission that would get him killed or anger God and that was the last thing they all needed after the victory they had won this week, and the victories they were going to need in the weeks to follow.

They needed Darryl. They couldn't lose him now.

When Emie came rushing to his side, he had to watch in awe of her. Joseph took in a deep relaxed breath. Emie was home and safe now. He grinned at her and met her there in the bay and picked her up in a brotherly hug, crushing her in his arms.

Emie laughed as her brother held onto her. She returned his hug also and sighed into him. When he finally sat her down, she looked up at him. "I hope you needed something really important you know. Asher is coming down and he's not going to be happy being summoned by you already."

"Ah. He will get over it." Joseph grinned down at her. He noticed Cristina was leaning against the radio room door looking sheepishly over at them. He nodded to her and let her know everything was alright then. He watched, as she winked at him and went back inside the room.

Joseph looked back at his brothers and sister. "It's Darryl." He told them all. He willed them to understand that Darryl was in trouble.

"What about Darryl?" Asher questioned him as he walked up behind Emie and stood there.

Joseph sighed and tried to think of the best way to explain it to them all. "Apparently while you all were out there saving Emie, Talia felt when Darryl was having trouble, and went back to heaven to save him. Darryl's angry right now about it and doesn't understand. Honestly," Joseph said running his finger through his hair, "I don't understand it all either. This is all new to me." He told Asher. He truly didn't understand it.

"Where is he at now?" Curtis asked walking up to them all as he listened in to the conversation.

Joseph looked over at him and told him "He walked out to the beach. Said he was going to pray."

Joseph let them all see his doubt in what Darryl was about to do.

Asher cussed aloud as he looked over at Curtis. They both agreed that it was a bad idea to let Darryl go out there alone.

Asher looked at Joseph and then down at Emie who was looking up at him in question. She was sincerely at a loss of what was going on.

"Darryl is my nephew." He started to explain to her. "He's the reason we were able to save you. He got us the plane down in Fort Bragg and followed us to New York to help us fight.

"He is vampire now too." He explained to her. Then he started thinking about Talia and what she meant to Darryl so Emie would understand.

"Talia and Darryl were school sweethearts." Asher explained to all the Whitby's. "He loved her like no other. When she died in an accident saving him, he died with her. He wasn't the same guy we knew after that.

"He left and joined the Army and spent twelve years running away from home. Running away from her memory.

"Darryl never really recovered from it all. I didn't realize just how bad he was until I seen him at Curtis' funeral. He was still distraught over her.

"You mix that with what all he's been through in the army, all he's taken on his shoulders all these years alone." Asher looked at Joseph then, knowing he would understand this part. "Knowing about demons and vampires existing, fighting them and almost losing to them, losing his own men in the process, and then being turned into what his mind knew was the enemy…

"That guy is still a mess right now.

"All he wanted in life was Talia back. Nothing else." He looked at Emie then who was really confused now and finished explaining to her. "Talia is an angel. She was created by God to save Darryl, then to be his guardian. But she was struck down trying to protect him during a fight. She should have died, but instead God allowed her to return to Darryl. He showed Darryl what he needed of him, the help we needed, and he allowed Talia to live."

Asher looked at Curtis, then to everyone else. "He needs us right now. All of us. Whether he wants us or not. We have to save him from himself."

Everyone agreed with him.

Emie thought about it all more. She understood now. She looked up at Asher then: her love, her life. She would have done the same thing Talia had done.

Quietly she spoke up and interrupted the others. "He needs me."

Everyone around her, including Asher, quieted and looked at her. They all knew it too. Emie had the ability unlike any of them to heal the broken hearted. She could help Darryl understand and see the truth. She could ease his pain too.

Emie took a deep breath. She didn't know Darryl very well, but she owed him her life. She reached out for Asher's hand and smiled up at him. "Take me to him?"

Asher looked down at the woman he loved so much. He turned his head sideways and grinned at her. "As you wish, sweetheart." He winked.

Darryl ran and paced on the beach sands. He couldn't bring himself to pray. He didn't know what to ask for. All he knew was Talia was gone, again, and he didn't understand why.

He stopped and waited in the silence with his hands on his hips. He bowed his head and let his mind run around all the ways this new life could be of use to him. He fought against demons in his own mind now that lied to him and brought him hatred and anger he thought he needed. They were big enough to matter, but small enough to make him realize they weren't real.

His stress disorder he had battled for years as a human, filled him now, and threatened to overtake his mind down into the darkness. Down into a pit he didn't want to fall in.

He heard the words that Joseph had told him before about how turning toward evil could drown them. How following it could swallow them up and they would lose their own souls.

It was when his heart felt tired from trying to listen to everything that his mind couldn't understand anymore, that he was filled with the images that haunted his soul in the past.

Talia. He could see her. He could feel her. He needed her. He wanted her.

He could feel that tremble on his skin he had missed two days ago, and this time he raised his head and closed his eyes knowing what it was and wishing he would have paid attention to it. He had felt it so many times before as a man, and he had felt it right before he had fought with Axel. It made him look up to the heavens and made him wish he could die for failing her.

It was her. She had been there with him and he hadn't even known it.

Pictures of his past life without Talia started filling his mind. But now he could see her for who she truly was. An angel. His angel. She had been right beside him the whole time.

There was nothing in this life or the last that could give him what he needed or wanted. Only Talia.

Talia. Only Talia could bring him back to life.

Darryl stood there for a moment and looked at his reflection in the ice that had froze up on the shore. It stilled him. It was like looking into an open door of his soul. He wasn't the same man he had been. It made him sign in resistance against the power that tried to fall him.

He had a new life here now.

Darryl wiped a blood-filled tear off his cheek. He was stranger, even to himself now. He didn't want to be the man he had been or the man he now had become. He just wanted to have a life spent with her.

When the pieces of her existence fell around him like rain on his drought-filled mind, he breathed in a pain filled breath of emptiness that burned his lungs and made him close his eyes. He craved things that once he would have killed men for, but it was so soothing, that pain. It took away the thoughts of what he was losing again.

He knew he needed to drink. He knew what his body craved was blood. But his heart, his mind and soul, wanted so much more.

Thoughts of her woke him up from the nightmares of the war he was waging within himself. He could feel the helpless nothing he had been feeling without her disappearing. It was like she was breathing into his soul, calling out his name. But she was nowhere to be found when he opened his eyes and that killed him inside.

Darryl threw his body down and sat in the sand. He didn't understand why God was doing this to him. Why couldn't she be in his life like he was promised?

Why couldn't he see her now? Why couldn't he touch her? Why couldn't he have her? He wanted to scream all his questions to God and he wanted answers.

He looked over the lake and seen where the edges of the water met with the edges of the dawn. He made up his mind then. The dawn was coming, and with the new day his life could be over.

Just like that.

The sun would rise soon and take his life the way it had taken Talia from his.

Darryl could hear in the recesses of his mind all the answers he was looking for. Trust God. Wait. Be still. Have faith. Don't do this! It warned.

He looked up into the heavens and finally spoke. "Why?" Darryl shouted on a prayer. He screamed it again into the darkness and pounded his fist into the sand. He hated how God had left him out here alone, without answers again.

"You can't do this to me again!" He hollered, throwing sand into the frozen lake at the dawn. "You can't just take her away like this and expect me to understand again."

Darryl looked at the lights of the sun that were painting the sky pink and purple on the horizon. He could feel the change in the air and knew the new day was coming. He sat there in the sand determined to let the sun rise, determined to make God answer him or meet Him face to face after the dawn took his life. He surrendered to the idea and faced it with a determination that shook him to the core.

Darryl bowed his head and felt the tear that dripped down his cheek again then. When he brushed it off he saw the smear of blood on his hand. He knew it wasn't a good sign. He was bleeding with shed tears. He needed to be filled with the life of blood to stay alive, but staying alive wasn't what he wanted.

"Save me Talia." He whispered looking down at his hands he was resting on his knees.

When she didn't answer him, he knew he had to have her back, or he was going to die, he told himself. He wasn't going to live another day without her. He couldn't stop loving her. He didn't know how.

Darryl closed his eyes then and waited. He was breaking inside, dying already. But he smiled at it. He knew soon he would see her again. He would be alright then.

"We can't let you do that Darryl."

Darryl turned swiftly at the voice of his uncle and seen the family that stood next to him. He let out a slow growl and looked back over at the lake. He needed only a few more minutes and the sun would rise.

Joseph spoke up then, leaning against the pier wall that separated them from the sandy shore. "The sun is not going to rise until you stop. We can't let you do this."

Darryl looked next to Joseph then and seen Cristina standing there. They were using her abilities to thwart his plans.

Again, Darryl growled and bared his fangs at them. How dare they do this to him, he thought impatiently.

"It's my fucking decision!" He hollered at them all.

Darryl knew Cristina had the power to stop time, he knew they all had the power to stop him. "I can't- I won't! You don't understand!" He said louder to them this time. He couldn't do this anymore. He couldn't live without her.

He was hurting, trying not to face reality. "I won't." He said again quieter.

Darryl turned his face away from theirs and looked down at his knees.

Joseph hopped the wall and stood there next to him with Cristina, his brothers Jeremy and Jordy, Emie and Asher and Curtis and Shelley also.

Cristina had stopped the sun from rising and was holding it there.

Emie knelt down next to Darryl who was still towering over her with his height in the sand. For a split second, she marveled at the man he was, knowing he was related to Asher.

She had yet to thank him for all he had done for her. She felt now was the time to do just that.

"We haven't met yet Darryl. My name is Emie." She smiled at him even though he wasn't looking at her and gently introduced herself to him. While she did so, she let her ability seep into his soul. She washed away his fears and cleansed his mind of all the hurting that was killing him and whispered to him, "You saved me, let me save you."

Darryl looked up from the sand and into the eyes of the woman who had passed him at Curtis' funeral. He had thought her the enemy then.

He looked up at Asher, then at Curtis. So much had changed. He remembered the life he had been leading then. It had been a life without Talia.

Darryl looked back at his knees then. He knew Emie was going to try to change his mind, he could feel her trying to do it, but he knew his will was stronger than anything she could do. Everyone was just going to have to understand that.

Emie felt as Darryl resisted her. She told him "Out of every one here Darryl, I can tell you assuredly, that we all know what you are feeling right now in this moment." Emie looked back up at her family lovingly. She knew they understood what Darryl was going through. They had been through it in one way or another. They had all loved and lost before.

"Love is a powerful drug Darryl. It's an unending feeling. It never dies. It's never stated. And when that love is lost, it can crush a person's soul. Destroy their life.

"But hope," Emie tried to tell Darryl's mind as she looked and placed her small hand on his hard, steel arm, "hope is just as powerful. Darryl you need hope. You need something to hope for."

She looked back at Darryl and told him, "Right now, right here with you, we want to help you. And we won't leave you until we do." she whispered to him the last.

Darryl shook his head no. "I won't, I have to go."

"You don't have to go Darryl. You just have to have a little faith." Emie said quietly.

Darryl bowed his head then and let the blood tears that were filling his eyes fill his mouth as it pooled. He knew those words were loaded. They had been said to him before. The power of those little words snapped his stubbornness in half.

Emie smiled knowingly at Darryl. She stood then to give him a moment.

Asher stepped forward then. He put his hand on his nephew's back. "This is what family is for man. To stand beside you, to fight with you. To show you that you will never be alone Darryl."

Darryl looked ashamedly away from them all. He stood up then. He ran his hands through his thick black hair and turned to face the dawn with his hands on his hips. Something in his mind reminded him of Talia then, and he could have sworn he felt the arms of Talia wrap around the front of him through his wings and he closed his eyes then and watched as her wings wrapped around his and pulled him into a tight angelic embrace.

But it was a dream. It wasn't real.

He bent his head and put his hands on his mouth to stop the pain he felt in his weeping. It was going to be hard, but he had to let go of the hate and the anger then.

"I used to dream of moments like that with Talia." He told them all, of his day dream he had. "It hurt like hell when I did it," And it still did now, he told himself. "But I used to wonder what it would be like to hold her one more time. Just to be able to look in her eyes and know that she was real again." He had to sigh away all the hurting emotions that made his voice struggle, but as soon as he spoke again they shook him. "I just don't know how to live with that hurt again, day after damn day."

There was a touch on his shoulder that stopped his thoughts. Darryl turned to look at Joseph who was standing next to him. Darryl noticed he was smiling out over the lake.

Darryl turned and followed his gaze. There was a man out on the lake walking on the water. Darryl tried to look but the sun had risen in the distance and he had to shield his eyes from the sun.

Then it hit him. The sun had risen. And they were all standing there being bathed in it.

Joseph turned and looked at his family. They knew who it was and what had happened too.

"Darryl." A voice beckoned through the morning around them all.

Darryl looked out into the water, not knowing what he should do. He looked at Joseph then for answers.

"Just start walking Darryl. Faith will get you there." Joseph told him in a whisper nodding toward the man walking on the water.

Darryl looked back at the lake and started walking on the frozen water in front of him in Lake Erie.

Every time he got close enough to the man, he found himself further away from the man. He was past the lighthouse now, clear past the sister islands out in Lake Erie. He stopped in the midst of the early morning sun, surprised by the light of the day on his shiny skin. He looked up then and there was nobody on the water with him any longer.

Darryl stuffed his hands in his pocket then and let his faith hold him above the lake beneath him. He took a deep breath of the misty morning. He looked toward the heaven then in wonder.

A voice, one filled with power and might, broke through the clouds above him and drove him to his knees there on the water. He looked at the water as he found himself there on it. He could see the waves moving under the ice beneath him.

"I did not take her from you Darryl." God stated simply above him.

"Your love, my creation, has been taken from me. Stolen from my hands. Cut down by an enemy, again. Much stronger than you, but not I.

"I have a new mission for you Darryl."

Darryl knew his mission without being told. He was bowing down as the words of God were being spoken, but he was ready to run in any direction to save her.

"She was running to you..."

And that's when Darryl heard the definite pause of God. In one moment Darryl was cursing the enemy, and then, in one split second he felt like God was cursing him with those little words 'She was running to you'. Like He was saying it was all Darryl's fault.

Darryl felt it, and he felt ashamed of it. It made him close his eyes and bow his head lower than it already was.

"She was running to you and wouldn't listen to me."

There it was again, Darryl thought. "Just tell me how to save her, please!" He begged. "You can have my life, you can destroy me! Just let me save her."

And then he heard God sigh. It took Darryl a moment to realize what it meant.

"I've been waiting for a hero like you Darryl."

Darryl had closed his eyes in pleading want when he begged God for her life. When he heard the voice that was no longer in the clouds but was right next to him, he opened his eyes and looked at the bare feet standing next to him on the ice with nail prints in them. It was his savior. His savior was the real hero.

"How could you call me that? After all I've done, after all I've thought?" And with that he squeezed his eyes shut again in shame.

"Because Darryl. No greater love hath any man than the man who would lie down his life for another. I was willing to do that for you because you are willing to do that for her."

Darryl sighed greatly. He was forgiven. He was pardon for his sins because of love. Not just for the love he felt for Talia, but because of the honest love he felt deep inside of him for God and His savior. He had felt it all along, it had just been clouded by hurt and pain.

"I will give you what I promised you Darryl. I will give her to you again. But I need you to save her. I need you to fight your way through this war to her. To fight until you find her. And then, then I will give you both a place in heaven where I will save you. I will guard and protect you there. I will bless your love in heaven forever more, Darryl."

"Well," Darryl thought out loud after the moment he let it sink in. "I like the sound of that." And in his heart, he could feel it. It was a heavenly freedom he had been searching for with her.

Darryl turned his face back toward the shore of home. "Just tell me where she is?" he questioned aloud in a whisper.

Darryl waited, and then he drew his brows together confused and listened more. There was no sound. He turned his head and looked back for the man who had been standing there next to him, but there was no one there.

When his faith disappeared in a flash, he sank in the waters below him. He struggled for the surface and when he broke the waves above them, he looked into the sunrise and stayed there.

He needed answers; he already knew the answers too. He sighed then and started swimming back to the shore.

Faith Darryl, he told himself. Walk by faith and you will find her.

And with every step of faith he took, he found himself walking on the water again.

Epilogue:

What better gift to give a hero than love? There isn't one.

Look for the next book in the 'To be loved' series and find out the exact moment when Darryl is reunited with Talia.

Made in the USA
Monee, IL
27 November 2019